Thomas Robinson, Heinrich Oskar Sommer

The Life and Death of Mary Magdalene

A legendary poem in two parts about A.D. 1620

Thomas Robinson, Heinrich Oskar Sommer

The Life and Death of Mary Magdalene
A legendary poem in two parts about A.D. 1620

ISBN/EAN: 9783337393571

Printed in Europe, USA, Canada, Australia, Japan

Cover: Foto ©Andreas Hilbeck / pixelio.de

More available books at **www.hansebooks.com**

THE LIFE AND DEATH

OF

Mary Magdalene,

A LEGENDARY POEM IN TWO PARTS,
ABOUT A.D. 1620,

BY

THOMAS ROBINSON.

———◇———

EDITED FROM THE ONLY KNOWN MANUSCRIPTS IN THE
BRITISH MUSEUM AND BODLEIAN LIBRARIES,

WITH AN

Introduction, a Life of the Author, and Notes,

BY

H. OSKAR SOMMER.

LONDON:
PUBLISHED FOR THE EARLY ENGLISH TEXT SOCIETY
BY KEGAN PAUL, TRENCH, TRÜBNER & CO.,
PATERNOSTER HOUSE, CHARING-CROSS ROAD.
1899

CONTENTS.

INTRODUCTION.

I. THE MANUSCRIPTS AND THE AUTHOR.

The Life and Death of Mary Magdalene exists in two MSS. of the first quarter of the 17th century, Harleian 6211 (p. 56—94);[1] and Rawlinson 41 in the Bodleian. The latter MS. contains the author's name, "Thomas Robinson," plainly at full length; the former his initials "T. R.", and his full name blotted out, but still legible. The Rawlinson MS.[2] contains another legend of another writer, entitled *The Life of the Blessed Virgin Mary*,[3] and has the following dedication to its *Mary Magdalene* :

[1] A small part of the poem, altered and modernised, appeared in 1869 (February and March), in a monthly periodical called *The Westminster Abbey Magazine*, or *Reminiscences of Past Literature*, which lived but three months. At the beginning is a foot-note : "This poem, which now for the first time sees light of day in print, was probably written by Sir Philip Sidney—it is thoroughly Spenserian in style, and will recommend itself in a very marked manner to the poetic mind."

[2] The Curators of the Bodleian Library were good enough to send the Rawlinson Manuscript to London for me, after Mr. E. M. Thompson, the Keeper of the Manuscripts in the British Museum, had declared his readiness to take charge of it.

[3] On the cover of the volume are written the following lines, by Edw. Umfreville, who has described several of the Bodleian Manuscripts : "Mr. Robinson's *Life and Death of M. Magdalene*, I have seen and read many since in MS. It is a very pretty little thing of about 100 years old, and, I believe, never printed—its age may be found by inquiring the time when W. Taylor was fellow of Trinity College." I did enquire, but without result. The Wood Manuscript (vol. 8490, f. 172), Ashmolean Library, Oxford, which contains a list of the fellows of Trinity College, does not mention the name of Taylor at all, nor could the College library give any other information from the archives on the subject, than that a man of this name entered the College in 1670 as a commoner. The words "To the Worshippeful," etc., seem to imply that Taylor was then an old man, possibly one of the senior fellows. There is no certainty that Wood's list is complete, which would account for its omission of Taylor's name. Moreover, the dedicatory lines do not specify whether Trinity College, Oxford or Cambridge, was meant. But the list of the college of that name at Cambridge (Brit. Mus. Coll. of Cambr. and Miscell., Vol. xlv., Add. 5846, p. 230) does not mention the name of Taylor.

" To the Worshippeful, his very kinde
Friend, and quondam Tutor.
Mr. W. Taylour, Bachelor of Divinity,
and fellowe of Trin. Coll.
T. R.
Wisheth health, and Happinesse.

When Socrates his sholars ev'ry yeare,
Brought guifts, and presents to their Master deare,
Among the rest 't was Æschines's device,
To give himselfe, instead of greater price :
My selfe (Kinde S') I can not nowe preesent
To your acceptance, sith I rest ypent
In Northern climat : but my image true,
The offspring of my braine, I give in lieu.
Deign but to cherrish this yong birth of mine,
A Muse it may be, though no Muse divine.
And thus much I with Æschines will saye,
In commendation of my ruder lay :
They that give much, more for themselves doe save,
But this is all I give, and all I have.

Yours in all duty to
command
THOMAS ROBINSON."

The Harleian MS. has, before the Magdalene legend, a Prologue[1] in heroic couplets in the same handwriting as the sidenotes to *Mary Magdalene*. Its last ten verses are addressed to a "great Lord," who is styled the poet's grace, and who is identified by the four lines prefixed to this poem, and scrawled over with ink, but reading as follows : "To the right honourable and truly noble gentleman and Lord, Henry Clifford, Lord-Lieutenant of the midle shires of Westmoreland, Cumberland and Northumberland, T. R. wisheth all happinesse and increase of honour."[2]

At the end of this poem are the words : "Your Honours in all duty and service to commaund," and underneath, instead of a name, is a long rectangular inkblot, from which some strokes of writing

[1] It is of course printed below.
It begins with some reflections on the difficulties that poets have in finding a patron, and also in choosing the subjects of their compositions. The various subjects of poetry are then analysed, and some complaints made, that poetry is not so much liked and patronised as in former days, for people are rather ashamed to call themselves poets. Then follows an enumeration of many Greek, Latin, and English poets, and, finally, the profit that arises from poetry is commended.

[2] Thus the author dedicated the two different copies of his poem to different persons, as Norden did two copies of his *Description of Essex :* compare the Camden Society's print of it with the MS. in the Granville collection.

project. By using a powerful magnifying-glass, I was enabled to read, through the blot, the name "Thomas Robinson," and thus confirm the suggestion of the Harleian Catalogue.[1]

To fix the date of the MS. it was natural to inquire the time when either of the two dedicatees was living. The inquiry after W. Taylour, which Umfreville suggests, proved entirely fruitless, as I have above stated; and the result which the inquiry after Lord Clifford afforded left the matter in so far undetermined, as the Clifford family had several members of the Christian name "Henry." Mr. E. Maunde Thompson, the Keeper of the MSS. in the British Museum, was kind enough to decide the point for me, after I had myself gone wrong, by showing that the watermark of the paper on which the Legend is written is such as was used in the year 1621. Perhaps it was also used some few years earlier or later, but the difference is certainly not great, as Mr. Thompson says that the watermarks about this time change very rapidly. We may therefore reasonably date the poem "about A.D. 1621." This date falls within the lifetime of Lord Henry Clifford, the fifth and last Earl of Cumberland.[2] Moreover, the poem contains (Part II. 1132) the line,

"There stood y* Monarche of this tripple Isle," etc.,

which is internal evidence to its date, as referring to King James I., to whom this epithet was first given; for he was the first monarch who united under his sceptre the three islands of England, Ireland, and Scotland.[3]

[1] "The author's name at the end has been more carefully blotted out, but seems to have been 'Thomas Robinson.'"—p. 243, col. 2. The Harleian Catalogue, moreover, mentions the two poems separately, as if they had nothing to do with one another. This fact has misled the editor in the *Westminster Magazine*, so that he did not find Robinson's name, and supposed it to be written by Sir Philip Sidney.

[2] (a.) Sir B. Burke's *Extinct Peerage of England*, etc. (b.) Dugdale *English Baronage*, vol. i. p. 346: Henry, Lord Clifford, Earl of Cumberland succeeded to his father's title in 1640. He was the last Earl of Cumberland, and at his death, in 1643, this peerage became extinct, as he only left one daughter.

[3] Compare Shakspere's *Macbeth*, IV. i. 120, 121 :
"And some I see
That two-fold balls and treble sceptres carry."
This is an allusion to the union of the two islands of Great Britain and Ireland, and the three kingdoms of England, Scotland, and Ireland, which took place at the accession of James I.

Although the date was thus fixed, and the author's name attached to the poem in initials and at full length, there was little or no chance to settle the question who was this Thomas Robinson. In despite of the most careful searches through the State Papers, ecclesiastical Fasti,[1] and literary records of the time I had access to, I was entirely unable to get a satisfactory result. The name, being a very common one, occurs, it is true, several times about this date, but unless he was either the Thomas Robinson mentioned (Hardy's *Le Neve*, vol. ii. p. 186) in 1615, one of the prebendaries of St. Martin's, Lincoln, or (vol. iii. p. 637) another Th. Robinson, one of the taxors of Jesus College, Cambridge,—I know not who wrote the poem. Except one line, Part I. 25,

"Poore, silly sheapherd-swaines? ev'n such am I,"

which may be understood to mean that the poet was a minister, calling himself the shepherd of his congregation, the poem does not contain the slightest allusion to its writer. So far as we may draw a conjectural picture of an author from his work, we have to imagine a man highly educated for his time; not only well versed in Holy Scripture, but also thoroughly at home in classical literature, and a perfect master of versification. Even the name of Lord Clifford,[2] which at the first sight promises to throw some light on the author's personality, does not do so. This nobleman's life is involved in great

---

[1] I speak of the biographies and dates of divines to be got from the following works :—1. Bliss's edition of Wood's *Athen. Oxon.*, 1813. 2. Hardy's edition of Le Neve's *Fasti Ecclesiæ Anglicanæ*, 1854. 3. Dodd's *Church History of England*. 4. Tanner's *Bibliotheca Britannico-Hibernica*, 1748. 5. Bale's *De Scriptoribus Britannicis*, 1557. 6. Pit's *Scriptores illustres Britanniæ*, 1619.

[2] The following few particulars about Lord Clifford I have gleaned from, a. *Court and Time of James I.*, London, 1848; b. *The Progresses, Processions, etc. of James I.*, by John Nichols (vol. ii.), 1828; c. Gardiner's *History of England from the Accession of James I.*, etc., Lond., 1883; d. Th. D. Whitaker's *Craven*, ed. Morant, Lond., 1878. Lord Henry Clifford, the nephew of the celebrated Earl George, was made Knight of the Bath. After having married Francis, daughter of the Lord Treasurer, Earl of Salisbury, he accompanied Lord Wotton on his embassy to France. "Earl Henry," says the Countess of Pembroke (Lady Anne Clifford), "was endued with a good natural wit, was a tall and proper man, a good courtier, a brave horseman, an excellent huntsman, and had a good skill in architecture and mathematics. He was much favoured by King James and Charles I. He died of a burning fever at one of the Prebendaries' houses in York in 1643."

obscurity, and he is but seldom mentioned in the historical records of his time. I was therefore unable to ascertain what his relations were to Thomas Robinson, or why the dedicatory inscription and the name were so carefully blotted out. Possibly the poet had changed his mind before carrying out his intention, or some unknown reasons compelled him to do so; at least his introductory lines to the *Legend of Mary Magdalene* in the Rawlinson manuscript:

> " My selfe (kinde Sir) I cannot nowe preesent,
>   To your acceptance, sith I rest ypent
>   In Northern climat," etc.

give rise to the supposition that he did not go voluntarily to the North. Possibly the later scrawler, I. W., who in 1682 disfigured Robinson's MS.,[1] smudged over Lord Clifford's name. I think it likely that Lord Henry Clifford never saw the poem. The lines:

> " What should I speake of those of latter yeares?
>   Of Harrington among our noble Peares?
>   Or of thy selfe (great Earle) the Poets grace? "

are noteworthy, because the Earl was the author of ' Poeticall Translations of some Psalmes and the Song of Solomon, with other Divine Poems.'[2] After all, the want of news about the life of the author is not so much to be lamented as one might think. If we could say this Thomas Robinson is the writer; he was born in such a year; these were the offices he held; he died when 60 years old: these few mere dates would probably make all we could hope to get about a man at this period, in which biography was not cultivated as it is now-a-days, as people were not anxious about registering all the little details of the private life of even great contemporaries.

II. THE POEM.

a. *Its two Parts.*

This *Life and Death of Mary Magdalene* is, so far as we know, the latest English poetical version of the life of that Saint; and it is most probably one of the last legends of Saints written in England. The late date of this legend is only intelligible from its subject. It is from its character that legendary poetry, describing the lives of

---

[1] See next page.
[2] See Bliss's ed. of Wood's *Athen. Oxon.* iii. 82-3, where specimens are given from the MS.—W.

Saints, martyrs, and eminent divines, developed itself always hand in hand with the ecclesiastical hierarchy. It flourished in the 12th and 13th centuries, when the Church after the Crusades had come to full supremacy over the State. From this time forward it gradually decayed, and ceased to exist when the classical revival and religious reform had shaken for ever the pillars of Church rule. But Protestantism, rooting out the worship of Saints, still acknowledged Mary Magdalene, because the Saviour himself had declared her a Saint. The poem is in eight-line stanzas, and consists of two parts, each of which has its own title. The first part: " Her Life in sin and Death to sin," comprises 107 stanzas; the second part: " Her Life in Righteousnesse," 92 stanzas. The manuscript itself is finely and neatly written, and is very legible, except in a few corrupted lines. On the margin, throughout the poem, is a concise abstract of the text, and now and then passages are cited from Holy Scripture, or from some classical writer, to which some of the stanzas refer. All the marginal notes are of a different style of writing to the text itself. In the Harleian MS. the first forty stanzas of the First Part show numerous corrections and alterations by another hand, and these are, in some cases, difficult to decipher. Sometimes only single words (especially in the rime), sometimes whole lines, and thrice whole stanzas, are altered. From the nature of these corrections, one would think that the poet himself had made them (for it is scarcely credible that any person would take the liberty to alter so arbitrarily the work of another); but their being of a far later date than the poem, proves the contrary. The original passages are much disfigured and almost effaced by the corrector. Underneath the dedicatory verses, between the words " Service to commaund " and the inkblot covering the name Thomas Robinson, almost invisible to the unaided eye, and, as it appears, wilfully effaced, Mr. Thompson found the initials I. W., and by applying a chemical re-agent to the passage he restored the number 1682. Most probably these initials and the number refer to the unknown corrector. At the end, as a kind of epilogue, are added 24 verses in Latin, headed : " De Christo cum Simone pharisaeo prandente et Mariam Magdalenam comiter excipiente." The manuscript is signed " T. R."

β. *Analysis of the Poem.*

Though the title of the poem leads us to expect a description of the facts of the life of Mary Magdalene, the work is purely allegorical, and touches but few events of real life.

After a short statement of his subject, followed by an invocation to the High Powers, that he may be kept refined and otherwise worthy of his subject, the poet plunges at once *in medias res*. The pleasurable surroundings of Mary Magdalene are described by means of a stately palace. This description (10/33) is entirely in Chaucer's style (*Knight's Tale*), and shows that the author possessed no inconsiderable amount of imagination. In this palace dwells a stately dame, gorgeously apparelled, and surrounded everywhere with all the rich treasures and stores of the known world. "Pleasure", for this is her name (11/65), rules the loves of men, and can make happy or unhappy any of her numerous suitors whom she may deign to notice or to ignore. Her attendants are numberless. Two voluptuous ladies bear her train; "Flattery" supports her right hand; "Wantonness" her left (12/89); "Foolish Laughter" paints her eyelids, and "Idleness, Jealousy, Inconstancy, Despair, Presumption, Envy," and "a thousand other graceless graces" are ready to realize her slightest desire. She strikes her lute, and sings a sensuous song descriptive of the pleasures of the flesh, and inviting her wantons to partake of them while life lasts (13/104). Then the revels commence; and here the poet indulges in the most voluptuous and realistic descriptions (14/143). Particularly to be noticed is his fine simile, in which he compares the boundless Ocean, receiving all the rivers and casting them back again in different forms, to the ebb and flow of the various enjoyments of the hour (15/159). Among the throng of revellers is one more lovely than the rest: she is Mary Magdalene (16/191). The poet pictures her as a being supremely beautiful, and goes rather minutely into her charms, subjoining the inevitable moral regret that such a fair form should enshroud so guilty a soul, or to quote his own words, that:

"So white a wall immured such worthlesse stones" (18/245).

For the favour and love of this beautiful and angelic woman, many rivals contend; but the simile the poet brings in here, cannot be said to be particularly refined or graceful (19/263). The suitors fight together, and the successful one claims the reward of his valour (19/270). The lovers then betake themselves to a garden, which is described as containing many fair flowers, "rich and rare" (20/303). The world of Flora has been ransacked to furnish a collection of beautiful plants, such as a garden of lovers should contain (21/311), and the result is magnificent; one almost feels the fine perfume, and can feast one's eyes on the blaze of colour. Here again the poet's description suggests Chaucer (*House of Fame*). The turn of his verse is often fairly happy, such as:

> "The Damaske-roses heere were brought a bed,
> Iust opposite y⁰ Lilie of y⁰ Vale:
> The Rose, to see y⁰ Lilie white, wax'd red;
> To see y⁰ Rose so red, y⁰ Lilie pale."

There are numerous other conceits of a similar character, which the reader will doubtless duly appreciate.

In this garden an arbour stands, where the happiness of the lovers is consummated (22/345), to their own shame and to the righteous horror of the indignant poet, who, generally ready with his moralizings, nevertheless continues his elaborate descriptions of what he seemingly deprecates (23/359). Indulging all these pleasures, and enjoying whatever can increase her sensuous cupidities, Mary Magdalene spends the best part of her life, only living for the brief hour (23/383). This opportunity the author does not let slip to "point again a moral" (24/399), although by doing so, he has not "adorned his tale."

From this life of pleasure, the Magdalene is at last aroused by the visit of a personage, whom there can be no difficulty in recognizing; it is "Conscience" (25/419). The poet describes her as possessing "myriads of eyes," having a knowledge of the future, and being the unmerciful Nemesis of every idle word and action. The advent of "Conscience" suggests to the poet an opportunity for a description of heaven with its spheres and different planets (26/439).

The workings of "Conscience" have their due effect on Mary, and she dimly begins to perceive the evil of her way (28/525). But "Pleasure" and "Custom" soon extinguish the glimmer of light, and she returns to her former estate (29/528). " Conscience " now changes her tactics, and instead of a good angel, comes again in the form of "a dreary hag of Acheron," accompanied with a " viperous brood " of torments (29/547). Mary is filled with melancholy and despair, and is hurried, and deposited with more force than elegance, before the gates of hell (31/593). The description of hell, as seen from the open gate, is, to say the least of it, original (31/599). Evidently the poet endeavoured to make it as dreadful and terrible as he possibly could, and he certainly has not failed (31/599). If making the blood curdle is a proof of art, he possesses it in abundance. Close by, sits " Melancholy " described as a man, and having a figure calculated to strike despair into the heart of Mary Magdalene (32/631). He has one peculiarity, which we hitherto imagined to have belonged entirely to the upper world; he calls for paper, pen, and ink, and wishes to indite a letter to his love (33/651). Afterwards his actions resemble those of a mad man (33/653). Mary is placed close by the side of this detestable monster, becomes his ape, and imitates his every action (33/672). Mary is thus allegorically described as being possessed of Melancholy in its most dreadful forms (34/687).

The poet then strikes out a new path, a path down a steepy way :

" *Wrapt all in uncouth silence of the night*," (34/696).

This second abode of punishment is as dreadful as, if not more so than, the first. Here " raging winter " and " parching summer " co-exist, and the poor wretches " frying, freeze," and "freezing, sweat " (35/723). Nemesis appears, and dispatches some of her subjects to torture Mary Magdalene exquisitely, but to spare her life (36/750). They accomplish their task thoroughly : she is led, in imagination, through deserts, over snowy tops of hills, and through populous cities, finding no rest for her troubled soul (37/783). The violent possession of melancholy and despair work on her like madness, and she fancies that she undergoes, in succession, all the fabled torments that the classic learning of the poet can bring to bear on the subject (38/823).

The first Part then closes with the description of the earth, given up to the cruel inventions of hellish thought and deed (40/863).

The second, and undoubtedly the better, Part of the poem, opens

with a description of the meeting between Mary Magdalene and the
Saviour (42/908). Christ is walking in the fields, which are adorned
with all the flowers of May; there he meets Mary, coming down from
the hills (43/915).   She casts herself before him, and the evil spirits
with which she is possessed, cry aloud, begging that they may not be
cast out, but saved along with all those for whom he had come to
die (43/925).   These evil spirits, remarks the poet, know the Saviour
and his mission, and thus reveal their intelligence.   The Saviour is
beautifully described in a paraphrase of the Song of Solomon (43/935).
After that, the spirits for a second time entreat his mercy :

> " *And hopinge, prayd ; but prayinge, prayd in vain* " (44/970),

but Jesus, with an awful voice, commands them to leave their habitation (45/974). His voice, says the poet, is like the thunder on Mount
Sinai, which "the nations of Salem" once upon a time feared (45/977).
Mary Magdalene, dispossessed of the hellish spirits, sinks down in
speechless gratitude and amazement, but exhausted with the fight-
ings of the spirits as they leave her (45/984).   Christ takes her by
the hand, cheers her in her tribulation, and tells her in well-known
words, to go and sin no more (46/1006).   Perhaps no passage of the
poem shows better the poet's style of workmanship.   He is nothing
if not classical.   In one stanza he is a Christian ; in the following he
has turned a thorough pagan, and Christ is styled "the winged
Perseus of the Sky," and Mary Magdalene a "distressed Andromeda"
(46/1007).

In a succession of figures,—such as the storm-tossed ship coming
into a safe harbour, and the weary pilgrim coming to his journey's
end,—Mary Magdalene is described as, at last, finding peace (46/1015).
She is directed by a voice from an unseen source, to go to the courts
of "Wisdom"; and there and then a dove guides her to the desired
spot, much in the same way as the star did the wise men to Beth-
lehem (47/1033). The ways of "Wisdom"—to freely paraphrase the
poet's gorgeous description of the forest through which Mary goes—
are ways of pleasantness and paths of peace (47/1039). In the midst
of this forest, the tower wherein "Wisdom" dwells, rears its head "to
the cloudy skies" (48/1058). Certain peculiarities distinguish this
tower from others ; and, indeed, it is no common tower. It stands

on a high hill; a rock is its foundation; thorns grow before it; seas lie beyond it; deserts with wild beasts lie on either side of it, and it is protected from the curious by a "thousand toilsome labyrinths" (48/1070). Like the castles of Chaucer, Spenser, John Bunyan, and other allegorical writers, each of these peculiarities has a hidden meaning. The castle's height represents Wisdom's glories, its rocky foundation her constancy; the thorns around it, the labours which must be overcome by the searcher after Truth (48/1065). The seas, the deserts, the wild beasts, and the labyrinths are its protections against unhallowed folly.

Humility, the door-keeper, admits Mary Magdalene, who stands amazed at the glories of Wisdom's dwelling-place. As she stands, lost in wonder, Wisdom reveals herself, and is described much in the words of Solomon, for whom the poet appears to have a great fondness (49/1087). Although the words of this description are almost exactly those used in the Holy Scriptures, Robinson has wonderfully adapted them to the necessities of his stanza, betraying no small skill in versification. In this tower, within the two rooms of Wisdom, sit Solomon and David, together with "the monarch of this triple isle" (*i. e.* Great Britain), on whom the poet implores the destinies always to shine (50/1133). Besides these, a numerous train of attendants await her pleasure. By these surroundings, personal and otherwise, Wisdom is allegorically conceived, not as a mere abstraction, but as a real person, leading Mary Magdalene to "Repentance" (51/1148).

"Repentance" sits in a "dark closet," clad in "sack-cloth," covered with ashes, and weeping bitterly. Unseen angels minister unto her, and catch her tears as they fall, in bottles (51/1162). The poet then finds a congenial task in opposing the results of tears and repentance. First, there is one stanza devoted to tears, their uses and effects; repentance is similarly treated in the next; while a third is given up to both in alternate lines (52/1175). A certain facility of imagination is shown in these three stanzas; and some of the lines are noticeable, such as:

> "Repentance, health given in a bitter pill," &c.

The Magdalene entreats "Repentance" to let her in (53/1213); and a dialogue then ensues as to why Mary seeks admission. Various

b 2

reasons are given, and at last she is admitted (54/1230). By various outward signs she shows her sincere repentance, and finds to her bitter cost that

"One ounce of mirth procures a world of pains " (55/1258).

She acknowledges her former sin, and laments that she should have been made so beautiful as to cause her fall (55/1263). Some of the stanzas which record her lament are remarkably good, and worthy to be compared with the stanzas of *Mary Magdalene's Lament*, wrongly attributed to Chaucer.

With Repentance, Mary spends some time, walks forth with her, and has her for a constant companion (60/1403). Mary fancies that all nature is acquainted with her sin; and this makes her lamentations the more acute (56/1279). She grows contemplative, and sees with spiritual eyes hidden beauties in the natural objects that surround her; and this contemplation is preparative to a fuller conversion (58/1359). She gets to know that Christ is with Simon the Pharisee, and she overcomes her scruples so far as to determine to go and seek her Saviour (62/1444); but before doing so, she provides herself with the box of precious ointment (62/1448). Then the well-known biblical incident that took place in Simon's house is described (62/1451). The poet takes the opportunity given him by this incident, to indulge his taste for hidden meanings. The glory of Christ is apostrophized, and the former and latter loves of Magdalene compared (65/1530); the parable of the debtors told to Simon is brought in, and various lessons, more or less useful, are drawn from it by the poet, who particularly emphasizes the rebuke which the Pharisee received (66/1551). Mary then gets pardon for her sins, and is sent away rejoicing (66/1559); and the true nature of her repentance is shown in her subsequent good life, and her great sorrow for Christ's death (67/1583). The poem ends with the description of Mary Magdalene's meeting the risen Saviour in the garden, and her joy thereat (68/1607).

γ. *The Sources of the Poem.*

Robinson's poem proves to be entirely different from all the known earlier versions[1] of the life of Mary Magdalene, not only

---

[1] α. Version of the Laud Manuscript; β. Version of the Auchinleck MS.,

with respect to the style (which would be quite intelligible from the different date), but also in the way of treating the subject itself. The earlier versions, without exception, treat of Mary Magdalene as the daughter of Cyrus, and sister to Lazarus and Martha. They describe her falling into certain evil ways in her youth; her chastisement by being possessed of seven devils; her salvation by Christ; her sincere repentance, and the service that she rendered to the Saviour in the house of Simon the Pharisee; and they finally speak more fully about that part of her life which she spent after her conversion in attending the Saviour. Robinson, on the contrary, describes elaborately the part of her life preceding the moment of her salvation, and only outlines the other part. He does not mention anything at all of her father Cyrus, her brother Lazarus, or her sister Martha. It is a well-known fact that the early Christian writers were much exercised in discovering whether Mary of Bethany, —according to John xi. 2, xii. 3; cf. Matthew xxvi. 6,—the sister of Lazarus, and Mary Magdalene, who followed Jesus from Galilee, were identical with each other and with the penitent 'sinner' of Luke vii. And this question, so often discussed, is not yet answered, and will most likely remain unanswered, as the Holy Scriptures do not afford sufficient evidence. Whether Robinson, as a learned divine, acted purposely,—being of the opinion that Mary, sister to Lazarus, and Mary Magdalene, were different persons,—or whether he thought it better not to mention these particulars on account of the allegorical treatment of his subject, cannot be decided. His poem gives the impression, that, by describing the illustrious penitent woman whom Christ himself gave as an instance of true repentance, it was more his purpose to point a moral than to make an interesting and minute description of her life.

Some resemblance is to be noticed between the *Digby-Mystery* Mary Magdalene,[1] and Robinson's legend. (The counsel of the

Edinburgh. γ. Version in Bokenam's Collection. I. Band, Koelbing's Altengl. Bibliothek. δ. Version of the Barbour Collection. ε. Version of the Harl. MS. 2277 (fol. 38 b), going to be edited by Dr. C. Horstmann for the Early English Text Society. And finally, ζ. Version of the Harl. MS. 4196 (fol. 157). (α. β, γ, δ, ζ edited by Dr. C. Horstmann).
[1] New Shakspere Society: *Digby Mysteries*, ed. by F. J. Furnivall. 1881.

devils, how to make Mary sin, and to serve them; her seduction by Lechery, and some of the allegorical personifications, are somewhat similar.) Nevertheless, this resemblance is not sufficient to give rise to the hypothesis that Robinson took the former as his source. Perhaps Robinson saw or read this play, or else knew another source of the life of Mary Magdalene which we do not possess. The accounts of her life under July 22, in the *Legenda Aurea* and the *Acta Sanctorum*, which were most likely to have been the sources, agree with the above-mentioned earlier versions, and are therefore out of the question. In my opinion, the style of treating the subject is Robinson's own original idea; his principal source for the Magdalene's life being the Gospels, and for his poetical descriptions and adornments some parts of the Holy Scriptures (especially the Song and Wisdom of Solomon), and the classical Greek and Latin writers. The marginal notes, already mentioned, cite in many cases the passages in question.

δ. *The Versification.*

The whole Poem is in iambics, the Introduction in 5-measure couplets, the Enchantress's Song (I. 105—142) in 4-measure couplets, and the Life is in Chaucer's and other writers' customary 5-measure stanza,[1] *ab abb, cc*, but with an added 6-measure line, *c*, ryming with the couplet *cc*. Robinson thus imitates Spenser in binding up his stanza with a 6-measure line, though Spenser's stanza is 9-lined, and rymes *ababb, cbcc*, as against Robinson's 8-line *ababb, ccc*, a form which Giles Fletcher the younger had earlier adopted in his "Christ's victorie and triumph in Heaven and earth, over and after death," Cambridge, 1610: see Guest's *Hist. of Engl. Rhythms*, ed. 1883, p. 668.[2]

ε. *The Style.*

In this, as in the form, Robinson has evidently made Spenser his model, and can thus be called a Spenserian in the true sense of the

---

[1] It is often called "Rime Royal," because James I., following Chaucer, used it in his *Quhair*. The stanza occurs in Old French before Chaucer's time.

[2] On Sir Thos. More's occasional use of a final 6-measure line, see Guest, p. 669, note.

word. One spirit pervaded all Elizabethan poetry, and although
Classical Literature has been at all times more or less the model for
English poets, and influenced their compositions, yet it never exerted
that influence so powerfully as in the 16th and the beginning
of the 17th centuries. A poem in' which—as in Robinson's—the
ideas of Christianity are blended with the mythological conceptions
of the ancient Greeks and Romans, in which allegory so entirely
prevails, and which is marked by such a profusion of classical names,
could only originate in a time, when the classics, brought back to
a new life, were so carefully studied, and had so powerful and
constructive an influence upon every branch of literature, as in the
days of the classical revival and the epoch that followed it. As
to the language, the poem contains comparatively few archaisms, but
is peculiarly marked by many words which one recognizes at the
first sight as the author's own coinages ; such as " ramillets, pillastrells,
turrulet," etc. Particularly to be noticed are his numerous *de* forma-
tions ; such as " deglorious, depurpured, debellished," etc.

III. THE TEXT.

As to the text, the Harleian and Rawlinson manuscripts differ
very little from each other, but the Rawlinson does not contain
any of those alterations which are found in the Harleian. I have,
therefore, as those corrections were evidently not made by the author
himself, restored the passages in question by help of the Rawlinson
Manuscript, and mentioned the corrections in foot-notes, where I
also quote the few variations between the two manuscripts. The
orthography of the MS. has been strictly preserved. The side-notes
of the MS. are set in Clarendon type ; those in the ordinary Roman
type are by Mr. Furnivall, who added them while reading the
proofs and revises of the text with the MS. during my absence in
Germany.

The Harleian MS. was pointed out to me by Dr. Carl Horstmann.
Both he and the authorities believed it to be unique, and neither
knew anything of its author beyond his initials, T. R. A search
through the Bodleian Catalogues disclosed to me Robinson's Rawlinson

MS.; and that, when it reached London, proved to be the same as the Harleian copy, save as to its Introduction and corrections. Saving Robinson's legend of M. Magdalene from oblivion, the present edition enriches the treasure of English poetry by another monument, and the list of English poets by a new name, although no particulars can be added as to its bearer. May it be useful to the student of the poetical spirit of the time, and contribute in particular to increase the knowledge of the development of the English tongue !

It is with pleasure that I express my thanks to Dr. Horstmann, and the Authorities of the Bodleian and British Museum Libraries —especially Mr. E. Maunde Thompson—for their kindness and courtesy.

OSKAR SOMMER.

London, March 13, 1884.

ERRATA (1899).

Owing to an unfortunate oversight, the *Notes* (pp. 71-76) have not been revised, and contain a number of literal errors, especially in the spelling of proper names. Besides these, the reader is requested to note the following corrections :—

P. 71, note on line 52. The writer intended is more probably Sir John Harington (1561-1612), the translator of Ariosto.

P. 72, *dele* note on line 178. (*iarre* is simply = 'jar').

P. 73, note on lines 459-461. The passage quoted is irrelevant. The reference should be 'Part. 2, lib. 6' (which deals with the heavenly bodies, in two chapters).

P. 74, note on lines 759-66, for *montis* read *mentis*, and for *Gebennali* read *Gehennali*.

P. 76, *dele* note on line 1574.

The Legend of Mary Magdalene,

FROM THE

HARLEIAN MANUSCRIPT 6211,

AND THE RAWLINSON MS. 41 IN THE BODLEIAN LIBRARY.

———

(THE DEDICATION *IS IN THE HARL. MS. ONLY.*)

H = Harleian MS. 6211.
R = Rawlinson MS. 41.

To the right honourable and truly
Noble gentleman, Lord Hen:
Clifford, Lord Liuetenent
Of the midle shires
Of Westmorland,
Cumberland, and
Northumberland
T : R : wisheth all happinesse
and encrease of honour.

Where should a Poet nowe a Patron finde, How can a Poet please his Patron ?
To please his own, and please his Patrons minnde ?
Some, Satyres ; others, Epigrammes, desire ; Men admire such different things :
Some, Cronicles and Warlicke strains admire ; 4
Others, a deepe conceited Pastorall,
Or Elegiacks at a funerall :
Some are halfe rauish'd with a Tragicke style,
Others affect the gentler Comicke smile : 8
Some one perhaps (and not without desart) some, Hero and Leander ;
Likes Heros hand and yonge Læanders heart,
Sung by diuine Musæus in a story
Of loue-sicke passion, worthy of all glory : 12
Others, an Emblem or quaint Epitaphe, [leaf 53, back]
Or merry mad conceipts, to make one laugh :
Some loue diuiner poems, and in this, " others, Divine poems ;
Deserue to be commended ; but they misse 16
In makinge a iudicious choyce : For why,
With painted flowers of Ethnicke Poetry,
Good matters (say they) must not be endited,
But rather in plaine easy termes recited : 20
Others, regardlesse of the Muses dity,[1] others, like Plato, despise Poetry.
With Plato banish Poets from their city,

[1] Corrected by a much later hand to 'ditty.'

Because they are too vulgar, and no kinde
Of Poetry whats'e'r can please their minde :   24
In faire Encomiasticks to commend,
They count it flattery ; to reprehend
In sharpe-fang'd Satyres, is to libellize,
To raise vile slaunders, and false infamies :   28

They condemn
comedies.

Base, the Comœdian's witty mirth *they deeme,*
And Epigrammes, phantasticall *doe seeme :*
Thees are a sect, of which most men partake,
That lifle reckonning of the Muses make.   32

The Brazen Age
has come back.

The brazen age is nowe return'd agen,
And hath defac'd the Poets siluer pen ;
Whereas in former time, the greatest men
Were not asham'd to be call'd Poets then :   36

Yet of old,
Poets flourished.

Witnesse Augustus, in whose Laureat time,
Learning and liberall arts were in their prime,
And Poets flourish'd : Persius (though a Knight)
Was not ashamed, Satyres to recite ;   40

[leaf 54]

Propertius, borne of enobled race,
T'indite Elegies, thought it no disgrace.
And sweet Amphion, sonne to princely Ioue,
With his shrill Musicke made the stones to moue.   44
Nor did this art moue onely in their sphœre :
An Helicon hath not been wanting heere.
Then sent forth Cydney, glory of his time,

Chaucer and

And Chaucer, auld, who for his au*n*tient rythme   48

29 and 30. The rime is altered thus by the corrector of H :
doth seeme—they deeme.
    32. Altered by the Corrector of H. to 'little.'
    41—42. nearly blotted out.
    43—44. crossed through.
    46. *A.* Corrector. ? MS. An, or One.
    47—48. altered by H. Corrector as follows :
        Witness great Sydney, glory of his time,
        Chaucer and Spenser, who for his ancient rythme, etc.
In despite of this alteration, line 50 reads "his memory." This
correction shows distinctly that he who revised the poems was
quite ignorant about the date of their origin ; Robertson is not
likely to have seen any poetry of Spenser and Sydney. The
name "Cydney", which occurs in the original passage, can only

Obtein'd a monument of lasting praise,
That kept his memory to thees our dayes.
What should I speake of those of latter yeares?
Of Harrington *among our* noble Peares?   52   Harrington won praise.
Or of thy selfe (great *Earle*) the Poets grace?
Why then should Poets be esteem'd so base?—   Why are Poets now despised because they're poor?
Because their pouerty o'rcloudes their witt,
And makes men rather scorne, then pity it?   56
Shall vertue, which in riche men we adore,
Be e'r the worse esteemed in the poore?
Or can not some mens honours credite lend,
To that, which others meannesse doth offend?— ·   60
Beside, I might recount in ample wise,   Poetry profits:
The pr*ofites* that from Poetry arrise.
Where each thinge, truly acted, we may see,
As in a theatre : Aratus, he   64
Shewes vs *the* p[*rc*]*s*[*ences*] *of* spangled starres ;
And Lucan singes the broyles of ciuill warres ;   Witness Lucan,
Of loue, and louers trickes, Catullus tells :
With warlicke stratagems, *grave* Virgill swells,   68   Virgil, [leaf 54, back]
And makes his verse each circumstance betoken,
That one would thinke the matter done, not spoken.
Ovid is various, and in nimble paces,   Ovid,
The love of Gods, the flight of nymphés, he traces,   72
And well he calls it transformation,
For he [reuiues] again the [antique] fashion,

---

refer to Sir Henry Sydney, the father of the known poet, or to
some other nobleman, who can not be identified.
    51. MS. latter. H. Corrector 'later'.
    52. altered by H. Corrector to 'and other.'
    53. Sir. H. Corrector.
    62. profitts. H. Corrector.
    65. both spheeres and poles. H. Corrector. This alteration
spoils the metre. If 'presences' is the right reading of the
obliterated word, it is used for the figures of the constellations
which Aratus described in his chief poem.
    68. sweet. H. Corrector.
    73—4 much scribbled over by the Corrector. 'reuiues' is
only a guess at the reading ; 'antique' is probably right.

Transforming truth into a witty fable,
So to delight the mindes of the vnstable :   76
IIis seas of sorrowe, holy dayes, and rites,
Letters of passion, arte of loues delights,
In eu'ry kinde may teach the rude some skill.
Hesiod *giues instructions* to till ;   80

Homer,   And Homers lofty style would make one doubt,
Whether he better sung, or Hector fought.

Horace.   Martiall lends witt ; Horace, in sharpe essayes,
Against the vices of his time inveighes.   84
Empedocles, in verses did attire
Secrets of Nature ; and the Samian Sire,
Morall Philosophy could grauely teach.
But Chrysostome had a farre higher reach :   88
And wise Prudentius, with other Sages,
Haue writt diuinely in thees latter ages.
What should I bringe Poets antiquity ?

So also Deborah,   From Deborah, and Moses victory ?   92
What should I tell of Simeon, and Mary ?

and David.   Of Salomon, and Dauid, that could vary
Musicall notes vpon his well-tun'd stringe :
When the Angellique troopes doe praises singe,   96

[leaf 55]   And harmony, that nowe is brought to ground,
Seemes to begin amid the sphœres so round ?
Much might I speake in praise of Poet's di*t*y,
And make my gates farre larger then my city.   100
I may commend, not mend them with my pen,
For Patronage belonges to greatest men.
And more to saye were vaine : For Poetry
Liues of it selfe, though Poets helplesse be.   104

Be, then, my Mœcenas!   Yet some Mœcenases this age hath left vs,
(Though of Mœcenas, time long since bereft vs,)
That fauour learning, and accept a lay,
Though ne'r so mean, though clad in simple grey.   108

80. altered to ' Hesiod instructions giues us how to till.'
99. Corrector, ditty.

Amonge the which, since chiefe I reckon thee,

,Accept (great *Peare*) this ruder *r*apsodie.   Accept, great
Earl, my rude

¦And though no *Muse* I am of great desart,   lines !

¦Yet fauour graunt; because I loue the arte !   112

Thy better iudgement happily may spie

The slender twist of my sleight Poetry :

Yet fauourably take it in good part,

(If there want wordes, be sure there wants no heart,) 116 They flow from
my heart.

And shine vpon my Muse with gracious rayes,

So shall it muse to sonnet out thy prayse.

Your Honours in all duty, and

Seruice to Commaund,

Thomas Robinson.

110. Sir . . . rhapsodie.—H. Corrector.
111. Poet I'm.—H. Corrector.

[PART I.]

The
Life and Death of Mary Magdalene,
Or,
Her Life in Sin, and Death to Sin.

1.

The death of her that was but newly borne :   1 *The hypothesis*
The birth of her that longe agoe was dead :   *or subiect of the discourse.*
The life of her, whome heauen and earth did scorne :
Her beawty, that wast *erst*[1] debellished :
How[2] snowy white inveild the crimson red,   5
    And yet the lily sprange vnto the rose,
      Vnder his[3] spiny fortresse to repose ;
How sorrowe, ioye, and ioye *againe* did sorrowe close. 8

2.

How night disrobed of her sad attire,   9 [leaf 56, back]
Put on the glitteringe *stole* of brightest day :
How *dreary* Acheron did once retire,
And needs would goe vnto the milky way,
To quench his wild fire, and his heat allay :   13
    How am'rous heau'n earth, earth heau'n did viewe :
    How the ag'd Eagle did her life renewe,
And blacke not *to be dy'd*, receiud an other hue :   16

---

[1] The words in italics are those altered by some later hand in the Harleian MS. For *erst* the Corrector writes *once*. The stanzas are numbered in the MS., and lines 6, 7 of each stanza are inset, to bring-out the fact of the 8th line having 6 measures instead of 5.
  [2] 'How' altered from 'Her.'   [3] his—MS. altered.
   8. againe—Corrector : original blotted out.
  10. leams (or beams).—H. Corrector.
  11. pitchy.—H. Corrector.
  16. MS. altered, seemingly from 'bee dyed.'

3.

The authors
invocation.

This *bee* the dity of my oaten reed,   17
Too meane (alas !) such mysteries to tell :
Yet heauens mirrour daine mee this one meed !
In earthen vessels, heau'nly soules may dwell,
And sandy caskets oft invest the pearle :   21
  Æthereall states, and high Angellique traines,
    (Blest bee the time !) haue sometime tooke yᵉ paines
To visit Abells sonnes, poore, silly sheapheard-swaines.

4.

I pray that I

, Poore, silly sheapheard-swaines ! eu'n such am I :   25
(Farre bee prœsumption from an humble minde !)
I will not, (oh, I dare not,) soare too highe,
Least hee, that all enlightens, strike mee blinde :

may be enabled
to write of Mary.

Sooth, this is all I craue, to be refind,   29·
  So to endite a laye with siluer pen,
    Of Mary, and of Marys sonne : and then
Her life, his loue declare, her loue, and life agen.   32

5.

[leaf 57]
The narration of
Mary Magda-
lenes life
described by
yᵉ Palace of
Pleasure,
whither shee
retaind.

Vnder th' Appendix of a hillocke small,   33
A stately palace *in a dale* was plac't,
Fairely incircled with a marble wall,
And with a court of shininge Amber grac't.
The Chrystall windowes too, were interchast   37
  With Iacynths, Diamonds, and Sappheirs blew[e] :
    Too happy treasure for so damn'd a crewe,
That newe sins hoary make, and ould sins *aye* renewe. 40

6.

Pleasure
poetically

The squared *greeces* were of beaten gould,   41
(Oh might it euer thus bee trod on ground !)

---

17. is.—H. Corrector.   19. heauens. ? MS.
22. ? MS. Æthercall.   R. spells "Angellicke."
28. least = *lest.*   29. H. Corrector reads " truth."
34. H. Corrector, on yᵉ plain.   40. H. Corrector, soon.
    41. H. Corrector, steps were all.

Pillars of Iu'ry did the frame vphould :
Ouer the brasen gates stood Venus, crownd
With Myrtle chaplets, in a charret round,   45
   Drawn by two siluer doues, more innocent
   Then shee her selfe : in the same continent
Blind Cupid seem'd to shoote, and tender hearts *vprent*.

described by her
Palace.

7.

A turrulet tooke vp each angles shade :   49
Two in the middle stood, iust opposite :
The battelments of smoothest Iett were made :
A glorious out side, eu'ry where so bright,
The braine it dizieth, and dimmes the sight.   53
   Doubtles Alcides leaft his pillars there,
   Baccus his Elephants, and Sol his sphœre ;
While each was chear'd with ioye, and overioyd with
    cheare.   56

The Palace of
Pleasure
described.

[leaf 57, back]

8.

The nimble shaddowes skippinge here a pace,   57
Seem'd in the Amber courts to sporte, and play,
Like wanton kidds vpon some steepy place,
Or tender *lambkins on* a sommers day :
So doth Apollo's euer-sparkelinge raye   61
   Daunce through the heauens spangled firmament
   To solitary earth, so male-content,
And backe from heau'n to earth, in lue of loue is sent. 64

9.

Within this palace dwells *a gentle spright*   65
Soft, sweete, smooth, tender, Goddesse of all pleasure

Aphrodite
described.

43. Pillars. H. Corrector : the original word looks like
Finiales.'
45. Myrtle : first ' Mirtle.'
48. H. Corrector ' to taint.'   ? MS. ' vprent'.
60. H. Corrector "lambs upon a summers".
65. H. Corrector "A queen of loue."
66. H. Corrector cuts out 'Soft', and puts 'fair' after
'smooth' : 'sweete, smooth, faire.'

By her owne
beauty, wealth,
and suiters.

Amorous, younge, *faire* slender *Aphrodite*,
To whome the Lydian wealth, the Indian treasure,
The Falern wine is brought in lauish measure ;   69
   The Thyme of Hybla, and the Libyan flor*e*,
   The gemms of Tagus and the golden shore,
With swetest odours and Assyrian Spikenard store. 72

10.

[leaf 58]

By her apparell.

Aphrodite,
the Goddess of
Pleasure
described.

Aꝺout her head a veile of lawne shee wore ;   73
Her garments were of skarlet rosy red :
A goulden bowle in her right hand shee bore,
Wherein all pleasure and delight were bred :
The nations came to her *deprostrate* bed :   77
   Happy was hee, that could obtaine a kisse ;
   Vnhappy he, that of her loue did misse :
Yet, oh most happy misse, and most vnhappy blisse ! 80

11.

By her attend-
ants.

Two Ladies did vphold the Damsells traine,   81
Plumpe, pursiue Luxury, and quainter Pride ;
The one *streight* lac'd, and *boulstred in amaine ;*
The other in a gowne, large, loose and wide.
Both, nearer then the rest, went by her side.   85
   Easier it is to empty out the seas,
   Then her with clothes, and her with dainties please :
In flittinge vanities (God wot) so litle ease !   88

12.

Flattery,

Wantonness.

Her right hand, guilded Flattery supported ;   89
Her left, did fickle Wantonesse vpbeare ;
Foolish *dame* Laughter thither too resorted,
To paint her eye lids, and her browe to cleare.

67. H. Corrector 'beauteous soft, slender, as a doue.'
68. Lydian : first, 'Lidyan.'
70. ? first 'Thime,' 'Libian,' 'flore' : H. Corr. 'flower.'
77. H. Corrector "inuiting."
83. H. Corrector, strait—twisted was amane.
91. H. Corrector, And Foolish Laughter.

Idlenesse too, and Iealousy was there,   93 Idleness, &c.
  Inconstancie, Despaire, Præsumption,
   And Enuie, that would brooke no Paragon,
Put their worst garments of, and their best faces on. 96

13.

A thowsand gracelesse Graces more be-side,   97 [leaf 53, back]
Attended on her, ready at her call :
They *nowe* awaited, *but* for winde and tide.
Th*ey* launch into the deepe, hoist sayle *and* all.
"Come (saith th' Enchauntresse) *'t is our nuptiall*, 101
  Let others sad and sullen liue, while wee
  Swimme in the sweets of loue and iollity !"
So, tinklinge on her lute, shee made this harmony : 104

"Come, come, my louers ! make no stay !   The Song of the
  Let's take our pleasure, while wee may :   Goddess of
  See, how the canopies all ope'[1]   Pleasure.
   To entertaine our loues do hope :   108
  See howe the silken beds *'gin* swell,
  Daringe vs their pride to quell.
  Gold and Amber in their places,   By her charme.
  Bid vs come, and see our faces :   112
  The pretty pearle lends many a smile,
  The sparklinge gemms our sight beguile,
  While the marble pillars weepe,
  'Cause wee are not yet a-sleepe.   116
  Hearke, howe the musike doth delight,
  Of that yonge slender catamite !
  See, the snowy virgins white,   She has lovely
  Hands and lipps, and heart invite.   120 maidens,

[1] A later side-note in H. says ' See Proverbe Solom Har :'
    99. H. Corrector, only waited for y*.
    100. H. Corrector, Thei . . . with.
    101. H. Corrector, let vs merry be.
    102. all scribbled over by the Corrector.
104. H. Corr., Striking her Iu'ry lute.   109. H. Corr., do.
    111. their : MS. y*.   113, 129. H. Corr., y*.
    117, 118. scribbled over by H. Corr.

[leaf 59]

Thousand Hellens faire, I haue

and brave men
attending on
her;

And as many Troians braue ;
Richly they attired bee,
Onely to attend on mee.   124

and about her
everything that
can ravish the
senses.

What so'er the sence doth rauish,
Heere it swimes in plenty lauish :
Ioue to mee hath brought his courte,
And the Naiadës heere sporte :   128
The Dryadës their groues have left,
And haue stol'n to me by theft ;
While y͏ᵉ Cocheman of the Sphœre
Loues to driue his horses heere :   132
Neptune too, and Thetis greene,
In my palace may bee seene.
Neuer saile out of the land !
I can giue yee Tagus sand :   136
Neuer goe to *Colchos* shore !
I haue Golden fleeces store.
Shades, yee wander all in vaine ;
Th' Elysian feilds are in my plaine.   140

Let all take their
pleasure !

Then come, my louers, come away !
Let's take our pleasure, while wee may ! "   142

14.

[leaf 59, back]

This said, a thowsand prostitute delights,   143
Flewe vp and downe y͏ᵉ courts as bright as day :

By her excesse,
and company.

Gluttonie, to a feast her guests invites,
And Baccus, to the wine is gone his way :
Others more eager, ceaze vpon the prey :   147
    The tables richly were adorn'd with store,
    Of delicates, *not known in times of yore.*
Such, Cleopatra gaue, vnto her Paramour.   150

129. their : MS. yͬ.   131. H. Corrector, Coacheman.
135. saile : first 'faile.'   136. H. Corrector, ye.
137. Colchos.—H. Corrector.   ? Original word.
148, 151, 152, 162. with.   MS. wᵗʰ.
149. H. Corr., which scarse were known before.

15.

The chambers were perfum'd with odours sweet,　151   <small>Sweet chambers,</small>
And strow'd with fragrant flowers eu'ry where.
The Damsells naked stood (ah, too vnmeet!)　 <small>naked girls,</small>
The Flute, the Lute, the *Timbrell* sounded cleare :　<small>music,</small>
Flagons of wine were brought, to mend their cheare. 155 <small>and wine.</small>
　'T was hard to say, which had the most delight,
　　The taste, y⁰ touch, the hearinge, smell, or sight :
So ioye triumph'd o'r greefe, and day dispelled night.

16.

As, when y⁰ boundlesse, brauinge Ocean,　159   <small>Comparison.[1]</small>
Imbezilinge y⁰ riuers all in pride,
Receiues their waters in his ample maine ;
Some backe againe retire with curled tide,
Some through y⁰ mountaines to y⁰ valleys glide,　163
　Some struggle with y⁰ brine, and foaminge flie
　　Vp to the pauement of the valted skie,
And downe againe, as lowe as hell, they fall, and die; 166

17.

So soone this crewe dispers'd : some to their sporte, 167   <small>[leaf 60]
All the Goddess's
followers disport
themselves.</small>
Some in greene arbours spent the *liue longe* day ;
Some staulked round about y⁰ amber court ;
Others to gaminge fell, and such like play,
And heere and there a drunken louer lay,　　171
　Who, by his giddy, braine-sicke concubine,
　　Disgorg'd y⁰ venoun baite of raginge wine :
'T is sugar in the mouth ; but in the bowells, brine.

18.

Fast by, y⁰ Lapithœ and Centaures sate,　　175
Each largely swillinge in a full-crown'd bowle,

153. H. Corrector, Damsells half.　　154. H. Corr., Viol.
155, 161. their. MS. y⁰.　　156. which. MS. w⁰⁰.
　　158. H. Corrector, o're . . . dispell'd y⁰.
　　168. H. Corr., blistering.
　¹ 'Comparison' is in a later hand.

Til their tongues tripp'd, and spake they knewe not
what,

Some quarrel; And speakinge made them iarre ; and iarringe, scoule,

And scoulinge, tumults raise, and vproares foule :   179

 Downe goe the tables and the goblets *faire ;*

 The ruddy wine, spilt on the Iu'ry *ware,*

Seemes like a fiery comet in the cleared aire.   182

19.

What should I tell of all might there be seen ?   183

some are turned
into beasts. Some were transform'd to swiue, and some to Apes,

Such was the power of the enchantinge Queen :

With Circes virge shee could commaund all shapes,

Or giue rancke poyson in a bunch of grapes ;   187

 Or like Medusas snaky haire at will,

 Transforme yᵉ *wisest Atlas* to a hill.

Her Magicke knowledge good, but Magicke practise, ill.

20.

[leaf 60, back] Amonge yᵉ wanton traines of Luxury,   191

That in her palaces themselues addrest,

Mary Magda-
lene describ'd
to bee one amonge
Pleasures
retinue. One was more beautifull vnto yᵉ eye,

More faire, more debonaire, then all the rest ;

In colour and proportïon so blest,   195

 That, were shee but with softer sleepe alayd,

 Of virgin waxe you would suppose her made.

O Damsell faire without, but inwardely decay'd !   198

21.

The beauty of
her body
described by the
symmetry of
her limmes. Her louely tresses of embellish'd haire,   199

Kist her soft necke, and shoulders iu'ry white :

The Apples of Hesperides weere there :

So Titan swifte displayes his blazinge light,

On toppe of Rhodope, with snow *bedight*   203

 Her eyes, as blacke as Iett, doe finely blaze,

177. their. MS. yʳ.   180. H. Corrector, rare.
181. H. Corrector, fair. 189. H. Corrector, greatest Sages.
201. H. Corrector, of th'. 203. H. Corrector, so white.

Rowlinge about, and they that in them gaze,
Looke for themselues in her, halfe lost, as in a maze. 206

22.

What should I of her arched browe relate,   207 Her brow,
Guilded with smiles, and amorous aspects;
The port of quietnesse, loues chaire of state?
Aurora hither her bright teame directs,
And all the while her higher race neglects.   211
 Her fluent tongue, with siluer is betipt;   her tongue,
 And from the caskets of her corall lippe,   and lips;
Ioue may diuine Ambrosia and Nectar sippe.   214

23.

Her ruby cheekes laid o'r the snowy white,   215   [leaf 61]
(Why may not An*tiques* erre?) were the rare frame   her cheeks,
That curious Apelles brought to light:
The litle birds *ynchantinge* hither came,
To picke y° ruddy grape*lets*, was their aime.   219
 Her nose, for Venus hill, 1 might commend;   her nose,
 But to the pearle, her teeth doe beauty lend,
While her eares pretty gemmes, with louely lookes
   contend.   222

24.

Next her *debared* brests *bewitch mine* eyes,   223 her bare breasts,
And with a Lethargy *my* sight appall;
But *by and by the selfe-wild heauy spies*
Vnto y° centre of her nauell fall,
From whence they starte, awaked at the call   227
 Of her *depurpur'd* thinges, *heere* at a stand,

---

215. H. Corr. o're.   216. H. Corr. Ancients.
    218. H. Corrector, Inchantede.
219. H. Corr. grapes was all.   219. their. MS y°.
    222. H. Corr. do bend.
223. H. Corr. soft snowy brests enchant ones eyes.
    224. H. Corr. y°.
225. H. Corr. suddenly y° eyling [? MS] heauy spies.
    226. H. Corr. And does to th'.
    228. H. Corr. plump—it makes one.

her white hand,   Whither to viewe ye siluer of her hand,
And armes as streight as pine, or subtill Circes wand, 230

25.

Or rather cast a due-deuoted glaunce   231
Vpon the marble tressels vnder plac't :
her legs and feet.   But then her douelike feete themselues aduance :
On such, Dianas nymphes ye game haue chast,
And the Nereïdes, with nimble hast,   235
    Trippe vp and downe, forward and backe again[e,]
    Amid ye gentle murm'ringe of the maine,
Curlinge ye flaggy lockes of the Neptunian plaine. 238

26.

[leaf 61, back]   Wonder it is, mee thinkes, without to see   239
So faire a face, (*aye mee,* ye more her smart !)
And that her soule should so *deglorious* bee :
But her white
breast covers a
black heart.   A brest so white, and yet so black a heart ;
Her worst the *best, her best ye worser parte.*   243
    Can such faire hiues inclose such idle Drones ?
    So white a wall *in*mure such worthlesse stones ?
So beauteous a sepulchre, such rotten bones ?   246

27.

A ' sepulchre,' that caue I rightly call,   247
Wherein her soule so longe imu'd hath been,
Bound with ye fetters of a willinge thrall :
Yet she must be
brought to God.   And yet that sepulchre must bury sin,
And for Astræa make a shrine within :   251
    It cannot bee, but such a heauenly grace,
    In heauens quire at length must have a place :
But first the goodly corne must winnow'd bee a space. 254

229. H. Corr. whether.   230. H. Corr. Or.
240. H. Corr. alas.   241. II. Corr. polluted.
243. H. Corr. Her best ye worst, her worst ye better part.
245. H. Corr. immure.
247—254 are crossed out by the H. Corrector.

28.

Amonge her riualls *iolly* nowe shee sate :   255
Each sues for loue, and loue to her affordes ; ·
But hee, that strongest was, the conquest gate :
No other arte prœuailes, no sugred words,
But force of armes, and dint of *steeled* swords.   259
 (Venus, the Sun still followes with her light ;
 If Titan fauor *thee*, her rayes shine bright ;
If hee but hide his head, Venus is out of sight.)   262

By the contention of her rivalls. She loves the strongest.

29.

So may you see alonge yᵉ meadowes green,   263
Two sturdy bullockes, (hard it is to say,
Whither with loue, or furies flames more keen,)
Both this and that *infect* yᵉ purple waye,
And make yᵉ sanguine riuelets to play,   267
 Flie at each other swifter then the winde,
 And with yʳ hornes yʳ heads together binde :
The victor, Io gaines ; yᵉ conquer'd comes behind[e.]

[leaf 02]

So two bullocks fight for Io.

30.

Great valour, sure to goe into yᵉ feild,   271
And battell bid for Lady Aphrodite,
To whet yᵉ sworde, and beare the trusty sheild,
To win yᵉ fauor of some fœmale white :
'T were better for thy countries good to fight :   275
 There, if thou conquer, thou shalt conquered be ;
 If conquer'd, death thou gainst, or infamy :
Heere victorie is fame, and losse of victory.   278

Better fight for your country than a woman's love.

31.

The bloody broyles thus ended and allay'd,   279
Faire Magdalene (for so the Damsell *hight*)

Mary Magdalene

---

255. H. Corr. merry.   257. that. MS. yᵗ.
259. H. Corr. glittering. 261. H. Corr. her.
266. H. Corr. rush ore.   269. yʳ = their.
271—278 crossed out by the H. Corrector.
   280. H. Corr. bright.

Her louer for his labour *well appay'd*,
And all *aggladded* with his newe delight,

walks with her
Lover.

Led by yᵉ hand alonge yᵉ valleys bright :   283
   And, as they went, hee am'rous glaunces cas[t]
   Vpon her rosy cheekes and slender wast ;
And nowe a kisse hee begg'd, and nowe his loue embract.

32.

[leaf 62, back]

The glory of the pole did nothinge please him,   287
Apollos haire could not one glaunce allure,

He thinks of her
alone ;

Nor did yᵉ fragrant-smellinge meadowes ease him,
The melody of birds could worke no cure ;
So fond is loue, so dotingely dimure :   291
   The tender plants, and minerals vnseen,
   Conquer each sicknesse and disease vnclean ;
But loue, by the same hand is kill'd and cur'd agen.

33.

His sences nowe no frame but hers receiue,   295
And in his fancy eu'ry member paint :
His minde, both sence and fancy doth bereaue,
And they againe his intellect attaint,
To thinke on nothinge but his seeminge saint :   299

knows nothing
save her love.

   Her loue is all hee sees, or heares, or knowes,
   So the bewitchinge *oracle yt throughes*
About the *maidens* fancy, strange Deludinge showes. 302

34.

They go into
the garden of
pleasure.

Vnto yᵉ garden by, at length they hy'd :   303
Atlas his orchard was not halfe so rare,
Nor *Heloriz in midst of* Sommer pride :
Nor kinge Alcinous his cheifest care :

281. H. Corr. Was called, her louer for his labour payd.
282. H. Corr. enflamed.
287. H. Corr. The spangling Diamonds rays could.
301. (? MS. yt ythroughes.)   H. Corr. Delphian tripod
throwes.
302. H. Corr. Preistess.
303. H. Corr. The garden then at length by them being spy'd.
305. H. Corr. feighn'd Elisium euen in Summers.

Heere y[e] dead louers sprights reuiued are : 307
  Flora had empti'd heere her precious horne,
  With store y[e] beds of pleasure to adorne ;
No thistle heere was seen, ne pricle-armed thorne ; 310

35.

The Damaske-roses heere *were brought* a bed, 311   [leaf 63]
                                            In it are Roses,
Iust opposite y[e] Lilie of y[e] Vale :   Lilies,
The Rose, to see y[e] Lilie white, wax'd red ;
To see y[e] rose so red, y[e] Lilie pale ;
While Zephyre fann'd then with a gentler gale. 315
  The woody Primrose and the pretty Paunce,   Primroses and
                                           Daffodils,
  The Pinke, y[e] Daffodill and Cheuisance,
All in Perfumed sets, y[r] fragrant heads aduance. 318

36.

Sweet Casia, and y[e] yealowe Marigould, 319 the Marigold,
That when the Sun bringes forth y[e] Orient daye,
Her armes, in signe of loue, loues to vnfould,
But closes when her Paramour's awaye :
The Cullumbine and Violets there play, 323 Columbine,
  With Couslips of Hierusalem so nice,
  Sweet Eglantine, and cloues of Paradise,   Eglantine,
Rare shrubs, and rarer hearbs, and beds perfum'd with
  spice. 326

37.

Narcissus too, that heart enamouringe lad, 327 and Narcissus.
Grewe by a springe (a chrystiall springe was nighe),
Whose siluer streames y[e] gaudy flowers *agglad*,
Glidinge alonge, as if they faine would prie
Vnder the Veluet leaues, and by and by 331
  Into y[r] watry cells againe they start,

311. H. Corr. Of—there was.   317. R. Deffodill.
  318. y[r] = their: the contraction is not extended, as it usually
is in the Society's Texts, italics being here wanted for Corrections in the MS.
  328. 'chrystiall', alterd by the writer of the MS.?, to
'crystall '.
  329. H. Corr. make glad.   332. y[r] = their.

But with a gentle pace, as loath to part,
Leauinge y� tears behinde, in token of yʳ hearte.   334

38.

[leaf 63, back] The flower, mindefull of his former loue,   335
Declines his head toward yᵉ neighbour springe :
His sportefull shade, affection seems to mooue,
Vnder yᵉ fountaine water wantoninge ;
Yet to yᵉ banckes his tender rootes yclinge,   339
  The silken staulkes 'gan tremble sore affraid,
  Least once againe Narcissus in his shade
Should loose himselfe for loue, and in sad silence fade.

39.

Mary and her Lover go into All theese delights yᵉ louers' eyes *aggrate*,   343
But yet yʳ appetite hath made no stay :
Her arbour. Into an arbour nowe *at length they gate,*—
This was the *hopefull* Period of yʳ way ;—
An arbour, pleasant, beautifull and gay,   347
  Incompast with triumphant baye about,
  And farther in, yᵉ laden vines *y*sprout :
If Baccus bee within, Apollo stands without.   350

40.

The leauy pillastrells were neatly shorne ;   351
Its seats are of grass. The grassy seats, yᵉ eyes to slumber wed ;
The vaulted roofe, on ample *baulkes v*borne,
With Violets and Lilies was bespread,
Like th' Azure skie with starres *b*esiluered ;   355
  The floore with many a flower was bedeck'd.
  The Gilly-flower, and Carnation speck'd,
But Lady Rose, yᵉ other with her beauty check'd.   358

330. H. Corr. do clinge.   340. H. Corr. do.
343. H. Corr. do charme.   345. H. Corr. they arme in arme.
    346. H. Corr. Together walke.
349. H. Corr. do sprout.   353. H. Corr. pillars borne.
    355. H. Corr. all siluered.
356. H. Corr. The fragrant seat with flowers was bedect.

41.

On flowry beds y⁰ Louers heere repose ;   359   [leaf 64]
And nowe sweet words must guild their bad intent :   Mary and her
With smiles, with lookes, with lippe and hand hee woos: Lover
Such were y⁰ Dartes, yᵗ subtill Cupid lent,
Lustes wandringe harbinger, vaine complement :   363
  Faire ramillets and posies hee prœpares,
  With sonnets smooth, and garlands for her haires ;
And so with gentle pace, into her brest hee fares.   366

42.

What should I tell of those polluted acts   367   do deeds of lust
That followe wantonnesse and Luxury ?   in the Arbour,
Let modesty not meddle with yʳ facts,
Sith tongue and hart, in mischeife still agree,
And as y⁰ wordes, y⁰ actions often bee :   371
  Their descants nowe they tooke, and restles rest,
  And thought they were with ioyes of heauen blest ;
But night as blacke as hell, yʳ meltinge soules possest.

43.

The Sun peep'd in with his declininge raye,   375
And dy'd his paler cheekes with fiery hue ;
It seems, hee blush'd, and would recall y⁰ day,   and make the
The wickednesse of *Vestaes sonnes* to viewe,   Sun blush.
That rush to folly, but yʳ folly rue :   379
  And thou, my Muse, packe hence with nimble flight !
  The shame of sinners, 't is no great delight, .
For modest care to heare, or chaster pen to write.   382

44.

Thus Magdalene in Pleasures wanton courts,   383   [leaf 64, back]
Parte of her youthfull dayes did fondly waste,

360. their. MS yʳ.
366. H. Corr. And on her brest he slumbers, too too freed
from cares.   369. yʳ facts = their deeds, doings.
  370. H. Corr. for.   378. H. Corr. Mortall men.

Mary Magdalene
spends her time
in dress and
feasts.

Ioyinge in vanity and idle sportes,
To spend the time, y^t soone (*God wot*) was past.
Prœuentinge all her pleasure with her haste :   387
    Parte of her time in idle languishement,
    Parte in attire, and gaudy ornament,
And parte in frolicke feasts and banquetinge, shee spent.

45.

She walks;

Sometimes the palace walkes delight her minde ;   391

she lies in bed ;

Sometimes in silken beds shee *sweltred* lies ;
And nowe shee's vacant to her louers kinde,
And nowe the garden doth inuite her eyes ;
But by and by, her arbour greene shee spies :   395

she bathes.

    Nowe in ye springe shee bathes, to coole her heat,
    And waues her *plume*, to fanne away ye sweat ;
And cooler nowe, shee makes a sunny bancke her seat.

46.

So do our
fondlings wanton
in their youth,

So *doe* the fondlinges of our latter age,   399
In iollity their fresher yeares *d*ispend,
Treadinge this sceene, as 't were a silken stage,
But neuer dreaminge of a Tragicke end :
Can great Iehouah take him for his friend,   403
    That in his youth doth nought but wantonize,

and offer only
their age to God.

    But when ould age decayes, both cares and eyes,
Then to ye altar bringes his haltinge sacrifice ?   406

47.

[leaf 65]

Let none on Magdalens delaye prœsume,   407
Though (sooth to say) it was not very longe :

Yet life is but a
fading flower.

Life 's but a fadinge flower, a subtile fume,
A shadowe vaine, a shorte, though pleasant songe.
Then oyle your lampes betimes ! and in ye thronge 411
Of Saintlie Heroes, *enter heau'n* amaine ;

386. H. Corr. which (ah, too soon).   387. her : first 'his.'
   392. H. Corr. softer.   397. H. Corr. Or—Fann.
   399. H. Corr. euen so.   400. H. Corr. do spend.
     412. H. Corr. Saintlike . . run ye course.

But backe againe, wee no returne can see;
The Lions den lets fewe or none retire :
And though ye intricate Dædalean gyre   707   Entrance is easy
  Haue many portalls, easy to attaine,   to it;
    Yet hee y^t knowes how to returne againe.   return impossible.
May count ye countles sands, and make ye mountains
  plaine.   710
          85.

As Amphitrite in her larger wombe   711   [leaf 71, back]
Receiues all other floods and Chrystall brookes,
So doth this lake all hopelesse soules in-tombe,
And still it hath more roome, for more it lookes :
So many windinges there, and wandringe nookes, 715
  That, though all nations of ye world should cease,
  And fall together in a close-throng'd prease,
Yet boundlesse hell could ne'r perceiue his owne
  encrease.   718
          86.

There raginge winter euer doth abide,   719   Eternal cold is
And yet no showre, y^r burninge tongues to wet :   there,
They allwayes haue ye parchinge sommer tide,   and parching
And yet no sun, y^r frozen limmes to heat :   heat,
So doe they fryinge freeze, and freezinge sweat : 723
  And (y^t which to y^r gripinge paine and greife
  Still addes a newe supplie without releife)   and everlasting
Æternity amonge y^r torments is ye cheefe.   726   torments.

          87.

Hither came Nemesis, and left ye skie ;   727   Nemesis
(In iust reuenge shee tooke so much delight :)   Κατ' ἀνθρωπο:
Soone as shee entred with her maiesty,   πάθειαν.
The ghostes inuegled with perpetuall night,   enters Hell.
Stood all amaz'd, and trembled at the sight :   731
  Their eyes were dazled with her bright attire,
  But, o, they quaked at her awfull ire,
Freezinge with fearefull could amid the flames of fire. 734

                                              D 2

88.

[leaf 72]
Nemesis calls up
7 fiery Spirits,

Amonge ye blacker sonnes of Tartary,   735
Seu'n hideous fiery sprights shee euocates :
They came with speed ; yet durst not come too nigh,
Least, happily adiudged by ye Fates,
They should augment y^r chaines and heauy weights :
   For Iustice could not Stygian vassals brooke ;
   But terrified them with her angry looke,
And heau'nly maiesty in hell vpon her tooke.   742

89.

In thunder then shee spake, great silence made,   743
(At eu'ry worde shee shak'd ye gates of hell)
" Goe to ye earth, and seeke ye wanton maide
That erst in idle Pleasures courts did dwell,

Melancholy a fit
præparatiue to
possession.

But nowe remaines in Melancholies cell !   747

and bids them
torment Mary.

   Torment and vexe her ! take away her rest !
   Enter her thoughts ! fully possesse her brest !
But spare her life ! in y^t yee haue no interest."   750

90.

So hauinge giu'n her charge, awaye shee flinges   751
From out ye cauernes of aye-lastinge woe,

Then Nemesis
goes back to the
sky.

And postes vnto ye skie with nimble winges,
Where Iris by ye waye salutes her lowe,
And on her weeds sweete water shee would throughe :
   But ye immortall power gaue no consent :
   For though vnto ye poyson'd lake shee went,
Vncapable shee was of ye sulphurean sent.   758

91.

[leaf 72, back]

The Hierarchies and Dominations bright,   759
Burned in fiery zeale and zealous fire,
Soone as thees tidings shee had tould arright,
And all with her in iust reuenge conspire :

Zanch: lib: 4:
cap: 19:

The hellish fiends were glad at Heauens ire ;   763
   And though about them they y^r to[r]ments bore

Yet nowe more ioyfull then they were before,
The damned spirits scund'd alonge yᵉ Stygian shore.

The 7 damned
Spirits fiud

92.

Through sad Cimmerian [1] mistes as blacke as night, 767
At length to fresher aire they did aspire ;
Though dazled with yᵉ glimmeringe of the light,
They easily found out this aged Sire :
Swift was yʳ speed, but swifter yʳ desire,   771
   Had not they been with iron chaines confin'd,
   By him yᵗ greeat Leuiathan can binde.
Then let not silly Saints bee troubled in yʳ minde. 774

[¹ MS. Cimme-
riam]

Melancholy,

93.

Soone as into his cell they entraunce made,   775
(And soone they entraunce made into his cell,)
Leauinge yᵉ borders of the airy glade,
Within yᵉ Damsells brest they come to dwell,
And thither bringe they mischeefes store from hell :
   Scorpions, and flames of Ætna, to affright ;
   Madnesse and feare, with many a ghastely sight, 781
And malice (what more deadly?) like a womans spight.

and take up their
abode in Mary's
breast.

Iunonis odium.

94.

But then yᵉ haplesse maide (vnhappy tide !)   783
Incited by yᵉ monsters huge [2] within,
Runs maddinge vp and downe yᵉ citie wide,
Like to yᵉ top, yᵗ in his gyre doth spin,
When game-some lads with limber stroakes begin 787
   To scourg it round about some larger court,
   That fecches compasse, while yᵉ simple sorte
Stand wondringe at yᵉ swiftenesse of yᵉ boxen sport. 790

[leaf 73]

Virgil: Ænei: 7:
et: Hom: Il: ξ:

They drive her

95.

The stroakes adde heart, and driue it forward well : 791
No slower pace yᵉ maide is forcd to hie,
Through th' midst of cities, and of people fell ;
Beside, [i]nto yᵉ woods shee seemes to flie,

through cities and
woods.

² MS. 'monsters hunge', with (?) n of hunge crossed out.

Like to y⁰ Menades y† 'Euhœ' crie,   795
  And in the honour of y⁰ God of wine,
  Nourish y‡ sacred haire, and doe entwine
Their tender Iuy iauelins with y⁰ braunchinge vine, 798

96.

That girt about with y⁰ faire spoyle of hindes,   799
Their merry orgialls and iollitics
Aye celebrate, with mad outragious mindes,
And fill y⁰ great circumference of y⁰ skies
With hideous shouts, and vaste redoubled cries.   803

Mary wanders about, with hair dishevelled.
So doth y⁰ Damsell wander heere and there,
  Trailinge along her lowe dissheueld haire,
With fearefull fire enflam'd, and could with fiery feare.

97.

[leaf 73, back]
Nowe through y⁰ aire with nimble pace shee braues, 807
And on y⁰ top of snowy hills is plac't;
And nowe vnto y⁰ dales beneath shee waues,
And yet shee knowes no reason of her hast:

She makes her nest in deserts.
Sometimes shee makes her nest in deserts waste,   811
  And groaues become her den, with trees around;
  But litle it auailes to hide a wound :
A guilty conscience maye in darkest night bee found. 814

98.

Nowe shee is catchinge Cynthia by y⁰ horne,   815

Her fancy is disordered.
(For so y⁰ troubled fancy will suppose,)
And nowe y⁰ wandringe plancets shee doth scorne ;
Vnto y⁰ higher Cynosure shee goes ;
But by and by a newe delusion throughes   819
  Her pride as lowe as Phlegetonticke maine .
  So litle blisse eu'n in our dreames wee gaine ;
And for such momentary ioye, such endlesse paine. 822

99.

Heere a longe time musinge in mind shee stayes,   823
Conceitinge shee in Pluto's court remaines :

Heere flames shee sees: 'greater, my flames!' shee sayes;
There ice congeald ; but coulder are her veins ;
And all y⁰ fictions of infernall paynes,   827   She thinks she
    Shee to her selfe ascribes : dire vulturs rent   suffers all the
    Her bowells, Tityus-like ; and shee is spent   pains of Hell,
With longing for y⁰ fount and tree neare-imminent. 830

100.

And Sisyphus his stone, shee makes account,   831   [leaf 74]
Comes rouling, troulinge downe y⁰ hill againe,   with Sisyphus,
That erst shee labour'd vp y⁰ steepy mount :
And nowe shee must endure Ixions paine   with Ixion,
On y⁰ tormentinge wheele : then all in vaine   835
    With Danaus his daughters shee helpes fill   and the daughters
    The siue-like vessells, yᵗ y⁰ water spill   of Danaus.
Out at a thousand holes, yʳ taske renewinge still.   838

101.

Thus (ah poore soule!) shee 's tossed too and fro : 839
The deadly feinds, yʳ furious will obtaine :   The violence of
And nowe her body headlonge downe they throughe,   possession.
Into y⁰ brinish waters of y⁰ maine ;
And nowe in fiery flames shee 's allmost slaine :   843
    Sometimes shee liues in dens and hollowe caues,
    Sometimes shee has her dwellinge in y⁰ graues,
And sometimes on y⁰ top of ragged rockes shee raues.

102.

No freinds can now persuade her to abide ;   847
No bolts of iron can her feet detaine :
The spirits driue her on with winde and tide :   She is driven
(Where reason's failinge freindshippe is but vaine)   about,
Fetters, like limber strawes, shee breakes in twaine, 851
    And then vnto y⁰ monuments shee flies,
    Where, groavelinge on the ground, shee breathlesse and falls down.
      lies :
When (poore distressed soule!) oh when, wilt thou
      arrise ?   854

103.

Vnhappy seruants to such Fairy nymphes !   855
Vnhappy younglinges, that haue such a sire !
Vnhappy handmaides to such cursed impes,
That, for a litle sweete of vaine desire,
Adde paine to paine, and fuell to y⁰ fire !   859

The writer pities Mary. Vnhappy Magdalene ! vnhappy I !
Vnhappy all vnder y⁰ azure skie,
Had not heau'n pity'd earth, and life been pleas'd
to die.   862

104.

No cruelty is as bad as Hell's. No cruelty with Hellish, maye compare,   863
For, from this fount, all cruelty proceeds :
While bloody Sylla no mans blood will spare,
(The walles lament, and swellinge Tyber bleeds) ;
The Furies fury, fury slaughter breeds :   867
Eight thousand Romans, Mithridates sped
With one sad letter : and on bodies dead,
Through Vergell, did y⁰ Punick wight his army lead.

105.

From Hell, Perillus fetcht his bull of brasse,   871
Wherin him-selfe first learnt to lowe and roare ;

(The Italian Turk, and cannon, came thence.) Th' Italian Turke from hence deriued was ;
And army-murdringe peeces from this shore,
Were, by y⁰ Spanish frier, brought in store :   875
There Cain first learnt his brothers blood to spill ;
Herod, his endlesse fury to fullfill,
Had a decree from thence, y⁰ tender babes to kill. 878

106.

Fond worldlinges then, that make a league with Hell,
As if thees quicke sands did not all beguile ;   880
If so it were, y⁰ Scythians sure did well
T' adore y⁰ Fiend for feare, and those of Nile

To worshippe Ibis and y⁰ Crocodile :   883
   But pride and tyrany together rise :
   Since Lucifer 's debarred from y⁰ skies,
Hee in y⁰ ayre his stratagems doth exercise.   886

107.

Witnesse distressed Maries sad estate,   887   Mary is in sad
Who erst with worldely happinnesse was blest,   estate.
And liu'd in Pleasures affluence of late :
But gnawinge Conscience, deuoy'd of rest,   Conscience has
                                       turned her
Her shorte-liu'd pleasure quickely dispossest,   891   pleasure to
                                       misery.
   Her former iollity, tormenting thought,
   Terrour of conscience, melancholy wrought
That misery,[1] and misery to Mercy brought.   894

    [1] 'Misery' from R.   It is torn out of H.

𝕸𝖆𝖗𝖞 𝕸𝖆𝖌𝖉𝖆𝖑𝖊𝖓𝖘 𝖉𝖊𝖆𝖙𝖍 𝖙𝖔 𝖘𝖎𝖓𝖓𝖊

OR

𝕳𝖊𝖗 𝖑𝖎𝖋𝖊 𝖎𝖓 𝖗𝖎𝖌𝖍𝖙𝖊𝖔𝖚𝖘𝖓𝖊𝖘𝖘𝖊.

[PART II.]

108. (II. 1)[1]

Soe night with sable weedes 'gan disapeare,   895
So melancholy vanishd quite away ;

The occasion of Maries dispossession.

So ioy her chearfull countenance did reare,
So did the orient day-springe bringe the day,
And all the trees were clad with bloominge May : 899
    The gladsome wren sate carolinge ye while,
    And faine the Titmouse would the day beguile,
But vnderneath, the meadowes at y^r musicke smile. 902

109. (II. 2)

Why did the flowers blaze in wanton pride,   903
And pearke y^r heades aboue the tender stalkes ?
Why was the Mary-gold distended wide ?
Why sange the birds amonge[2] their leauy walkes ?
Why skipp'd the lambs vpon their steepy balkes ? 907

Christ, in his course,

    Certes, the welbeloued went that waye,
    The heire of heauen, from whose glorious ray
The Sun deriues his light, and Phosphorus ye daye. 910

110. (II. 3)

[leaf 76, back]
sees Mary.

And as that way he went (thrice happy houre !)   911
He spy'd a mayde come tumblinge downe apace,

---

[1] The numbering of the Stanzas begins again with 1 in the MS, but it is carried on from Part I in this print, for convenience of reference, as *M. M.* st. 108, &c.
[2] Corrected to 'amid'.

From toppe of hills, y^t to the heauen towre :
A hollowe voice he heard, y^t would aghast
A wandringe straunger, and the Spirits cast   915   The Spirits in her
  Her beauteous frame before his whiter feet,   cast her at His
    And boweinge to ye ground, (as it was meete,)   feet.
His maiesty with feigned salutations greete.   918

111. (II. 4)

Then with their vncouth hollow soundinge voice,   919
(Such language Hell had taught them longe agoe,)
They roare and crye aloude with hydeous noyse,
"Wee knowe thy name ; and whence thou art, we   The Spirits in
  knowe :   Mary ask Christ
                                   not to turn them
O doe not vse vs licke a cruell foe !   923   out of her.
  Thou art the Sonne of God, for euer blest !
  Thou cam'st to saue ; then saue vs with ye rest,
And dispossesse vs not from out this balefull brest ! 926

112. (II. 5)

"Wee bee ye harbingers of heauens ire,   927
Wee Mercuries vnto Astræa bright,
Wee punish sinners in ye lake of fire,
Wee giue thee reuerence, and homage right,
And dutifully tremble at thy sight ;   931   They tremble and
  While man doth mocke at heauens ofspringe still,   obey Him, the
  Wee yeeld obedience to thy sacred will :
Thou art a springe of good ; oh, worke not vs this ill !"   Source of Good.

113. (II. 6)

Wonder it is, y^t this accursed crue   935   [leaf 77]
Should knowe ye Sauiour, whom but few could knowe ;   For so hee is
Sure, they obscru'd his white and ruddy hue,   described in the
That made him cheefest of 10 thousand showe,   Canticles :
His lockes as blacke as rauen, and ye snowe   939   and the diue'ls
  Of his faire Doue-like eyes. His cheekes beneath   knowe the
    Bedight with flowers, like beds of Spices breath ;   Scriptures.
His lily lippes, pure myrrhe vnto his spouse bequeath.   Luk: 9:

114. (II. 7)

Cantic: 5: 13:

His hands, gould ringes beset with Chrysolite ;   943
His mouth, with sweetnesse fraught, and odours newe ;
His belly vnder, like y⁰ Iu'ry white,
All interchast with veins of Sappheirs blewe :
His pleasant countenance like Hermons dewe,   947
  His leggs and feete, like marble pillers rare
  On goulden sockets, yet by farre more faire :
His vestures, with y^r Casia perfum'd y⁰ aire.   950

115. (II. 8)

Christ's robe.

A robe hee wore, like to his essence, pure ;   951
That vndiuided ; vndeuided hee :
No wonder then (though 't seemes a wonder, sure)
That gloomy hell withouten eyes can see,
Iesus alone y⁰ holy one to bee,   955
  And y⁰ Messias, y^t should sin deface :
  Such was his countenance and louely grace,
That they bewrayd his country, and his heau'nly race.

116. (II. 9)

[leaf 77, back]
Zanch: lib: 3:
cap: 9: et: lib: 9:
cap: 9:

Though thought be free, nor can y⁰ Stygian frie   959
Enter y⁰ chambers of our better parte,
(For y^t belonges to heau'ns all-seeinge eye,
To search y⁰ reines, and vnderstand y⁰ hearte,
Nor will he this vnto his foes imparte)   963
  Whither they through y⁰ Sences windowes pry'd,
  Or this by reuelation espy'd :
They knewe our Sauiours thought, and what would them
  betyde.   966

117. (II. 10)

But thus y⁰ subtill serpents him bespake,   967
Hopinge, of Mercy, mercy to obtaine :
Yet simple elues, y^r marke they did mistake,
And hopinge prayd, and prayinge prayd in vaine :

For hee, poore Adam's sonnes will rather gaine ;   971
  " You knowe me, (said hee) but I knowe not you ;
  And yet I knowe yee for a cursed crewe :
Then leaue your habitation, and secke a newe !   974

Christ bids the
Spirits quit Mary.

118. (II. 11)

Like as yᵉ thunder on mount Sinai hearde,   975
With flashinge lightninges and shrill trumpets sounde,
The future nations of Salem feard,
And made them flie, or fall flat on the ground,
Soe doth yᵉ thunder of his voice confounde   979
    The powers of hell, who from his glorious sight,
    Swellinge with rancor, blasphemies and spight,
Vnto yʳ dungeon againe they take yʳ flight.   982

The dispossession
of the euill
spirits.

119. (II. 12)

Soone as they tooke yʳ leaue, yᵗ causd her thrall,   983
Downe sunke yᵉ Damsell in amazement deepe,
(After an earth-quake, soe the ground doth fall,)
And soundinge, yeelded to a sencelesse sleepe,
Ne could shee speake a worde, ne could shee weepe : 987
    But he yᵗ conquered all the powers beneath,
    The Hell of sin, and sin of Hell, and Death,
Soone brought againe yᵉ maydens pantinge, faintinge
    breath.   990

[leaf 78]
Mary sinks down.

120. (II. 13)

With milke-white hand, hee by yᵉ hand her tooke, 991
And stayd her faintinge head, and bad her cheare :
The burninge feuer then her heart forsooke,
Instead of which there came a suddaine feare :
So, when yᵉ night begins to disappeare,   995
    The dawinge of yᵉ day with glimmeringe light,
    That seemeth vncouth to yᵉ weaker sight,
One newly layd a sleepe, and new awakd doth fright.

Christ lifts her by
the hand,

121. (II. 14)

But feare soone vanishd, when ye heauenly swan, 999

and comforts her. With Musicke of his voice did comforte giue ;
And then to sue for fauour shee began,
And humbly craue y^t shee with him might liue,
That did her soule from Hell and death repreiue. 1003
 As yet he granted not her suite : but said,
 "Thy trespasses are pardoned (O maide) !
[¹ first, 'them'] Repent¹ thee ; and to sin heere after, bee affrayd !"

122. (II. 15)

[leaf 7£, back] Thus did ye winged Perseus of ye skie 1007
Mary is rescued. Deliuer our distress'd Andromede,
That nowe with greefe prœpar'd herselfe to dye
By ye waue-tossinge monster of ye sea,
The sea of Acheron : nowe Panopee, 1011
 With all her nimphes, scuddes on ye marble plaine ;
 The storme is ouerblowne, and once againe
Daye triumphes ouer night, and pleasure ouer paine. 1014

123. (II. 16)

The ship, that erst was toss'd with winde and tyde ;
Hath nowe ye port of quietnesse attaind ;
The pilgrime wandringe through ye deserts wide,
Hath nowe at length a ioyefull harbour gaind ;
And shee, that erst was pitied and plaind, 1019
The returne of a Nowe weepes for ioy, and ioyes in sorrow true ;
good conscience. And faire Syneide is return'd to viewe
Her chambers, and to build ye palaces a newe. 1022

124. (II. 17)

No sooner had she entred, but ye mayde 1023
Felt a warme motion within her brest,
And hard a tongue (though none shee sawe) y^t sayd :
Mary is told to "Goe to ye courts of Wisedome, gentle guest ;
seek Repentance. There seeke Repentance, and with her, find rest : 1027

Repentance hath a flood, doth euer flowe,
A flood of brinish[1] teares and bitter woe,
That, bee thou n'er soe blacke, will make thee white as
    snowe."   1030

125. (II. 18)

Mary, aggladded at this ioyfull newes,   1031   [leaf 79]
Seekes for yᵉ palaces of Sapience;   Mary is guided
A siluer doue, yᵉ way vnto her shewes,   to the Palace of
                                                     Wisdom.
And with his bill giues her intelligence,
Soe that shee needs no conduct of yᵉ sence,   1035
    And yet shee can not bee without it well.
    Such pleasure, by yᵉ way shee goes, doth dwell,
'T is hard to bee conceiud, but harder farre to tell.

126. (II. 19)

The forrests were like fragrant Lebanon :   1039   Cantic: 4: 11:
Pome-granates sweete, and saffron there contend ;
Spiknarde and Camphire with browne Cinnamon ;   Wisedome
Calamus, Myrrhe and Aloes befreind   described by her
Th' enamourd ayre, and all about they send   1043   forrest.
    Perfumes, exhaled from yʳ spicy beds.
    And heere and there a springe of milke dispreads,
And hony-dewe yᵉ sweeter shrubs of spices weds. 1046

127. (II. 20)

The riuers shind with oyle, and on yᵉ shore   1047   On the shore are
                                                     pearls and jewels.
Faire Margarites and costly iewells laye ;
The land emboweled great mines of Ore,
And all a-longe yᵉ tinne-decayinge way,
The goodly Cedars seem'd to bidde her stay :   1051
    These did her captiuated eyes delight ;
    The flowry beds detaine her feete so white,
And middle-sizëd shrubs her tender hands invite. 1054

---

[1] MS. 'brimish,' as below too, p. 54, l. 1232.

128. (II. 21)

[leaf 79, back] But then a rarer spectacle shee spies,   1055

By the situation of her tower. The tower of Wisedome, y^t did seeme to threat,

With highe-aspiringe toppe ye cloudy skies :

The ground-worke on a massy rocke was set,

That neither windes could hurt, nor waters great. 1059

Sharpe prickinge thornes and thistles were before ;

On each side, desarts waste, and wilde beasts roare ;

Beyond, a furious sea doth wrastle with ye shore. 1062

129. (II. 22)

Why standes it on a hill ?—her glorie's highe ;   1063

Why on a rocke ?—shee constant doth perseuer ;

Wisdom's Palace. Why thornes before it ?—hard aduersity

And spiny labour goe before her euer ;

Why seas beyond it ?—head-longe folly neuer   1067

Is farre from daunger ; why on eyther side

Desarts and beasts ?—if either way you slide,

Into a thousand toylesome Labyrinths you glide. 1070

130. (II. 23)

What should I of this palace more relate,   1071

That in it-selfe all beauties doth enfould ?

All there was pretious, and of highest rate,

And though all glist'red not, yet all was gould,

Or moulde as pure, or farre the purer mould.   1075

By humility her porter. Watchfull Humility still kept ye dore,

And none had entrance to ye courte, before

They crau'd her helpinge hand, and did her ayde

implore.   1078

131. (II. 24)

[leaf 80] Humility, instructions harbinger,   1079

Sorrowes glad ofspringe, mother of our peace,

Charities nurse, Religions fosterer,

Path-way to heauen, troubled soules release ;

Prides great abater, vertues great encrease,   1083
   Others by risinge, raize y^r high desires;
   But when shee lowest falls, shee most aspires;
Shee dulls ye sharpest swordes, and quenches flaminge
   fiers.   1086

132. (II. 25)

Magdalene entred with this happy guide;   1087
And all amazed at ye rasters[1] bright,   [1 ? rafters]
Stone-still shee stood, till Wisedome shee espy'd,
With her owne worke of needle-worke bedight :
Then while shee wonders, giue mee leaue to write 1091 By her own
   Of her, with whome ye Sun may not compare : personage.
   Doue-like her eyes; her lockes of curled haire, Wised: Sal: 7:
                                    29;
A flocke of kids, y^t on mount Gilead feedinge are 1094 Cantic: 4:

133. (II. 26)

Her temples, peices of Pomegranates seeme;   1095 The person of
                                        Wisdom
Her feet, like newe-wash'd sheepe, ordred arright; described.
Her lippes, a thred of scarlet, you would deeme;
Her necke, like Dauids tower, where men of might
Hange vp y^r Targets, all in open sight;   1099
   Her brests like two yonge roes of œquall age,
   Amid ye lilies that haue pasturage :
Her talke is euer comely, sweet her carriage.   1102

134. (II. 27)

Doth any, honours diadem admire ?   1103 [leaf 80, back]
With her, immortall honours euer dwell.
Doth any, great possessions desire ?
Her riches, fadinge treasures farre excell. Her riches excel
                                   all other treasures.
Is any thirsty ? shee 's a liuinge well;   1107
   Shee makes ye weake man stronge, ye foolish wise;
   Shee lends ye lame man feete, ye blinde man eyes;
Shee feedes ye hungry soule, and clothes ye naked
   thighes.   1110

MARY MAGDALENE.   E

135. (II. 28)

By her
properties.

Wisedome 's yᵉ best of thinges, th' immortal treasure,
The double booke of Nature and of grace,
Honour deuoyd of shame, and painelesse pleasure,
Pilot of life, and life of eu'ry place,
Nobles reiecter, raiser of yᵉ base,   1115
  Falsehoods discouery, light of humaine sence,

Wised: Sal: 7:
v: 25: 26:

´The great Allmighties subtill influence,
Mirrour of maiesty, heauens purest Quintessence. 1118

136. (II. 29)

Oh that I might for euer heere abide,   1119

[¹ yᵗ = that]

Within yᵉ palaces, that¹ age out-last,
And stay with Mary hard by Wisedomes side ;
How nimbly would yᵉ goulden numbers hast,
When of her Nectar I should sippe a tast.   1123
  Hence did yᵉ waters of Castalian plaine
  First issue forth, though in a purer vaine :
And shee, yᵉ Pallas is, of great Iehouahs braine. 1126

137. (II. 30)

[leaf 81]

But nowe, behould, a goodly company   1127
Of Wisedomes children stand about her round :   -

By her 2
chambers.

Two roomes shee hath, this lowe, the other highe :
Heere sate Prince Salomon, and Dauid crownd,
With thousands of his Saints in pleasure drownd. 1131

In them are all

There stood yᵉ Monarche of this tripple Isle :
The Destinies for euer on him smile.
Others there were, but fewe, or none appear'd yᵉ
    while,   1134

138. (II. 31)

Beside all those that fauour her essayes,   1135
Whom in her palaces shee highly grac't,

1122, 1123. In H., 'hast,' 'tast' have a final *e* put on by
a later hand.

And crownd with garlands of immortall bayes,

That soe y^r names might neuer be defact,

Nor by ye tyrany of time eract,   1139

> That they ye Muses with y^r fauour rayse,
>
> And, by ye trumpet of ye Muses prayse,

Out-weare all-wearinge time, and liue immortall dayes.

whom Wisdom makes immortal.

139. (II. 32)

But whither doe my wandringe numbers straye?   1143

Returne (yee Muses) to the path againe!

And yet, with Wisedome, well they wander may,

Better then walke right on with folly vaine.

Heere all ye while stoode Magdalene, soe faine   1147

> To meete Repentance: Wisedome at ye last
>
> With hand in hand (shee knew ye Damselles hast)

Conductes her thither, where ye weepinge grace was

plac't.   1150

By her inmate repentance. Wisdom leads Mary to Repentance.

140. (II. 33)

Streightly immured in a closet small,   1151

Repentance sate, with eyes still fixt on ground;

A-downe her cheekes ye tricklinge teares fall;

Her slender hands, her tender brest ywound;

And, (woe is me!) shee cries with sighinge sound: 1155

> Her carelesse-hanginge haire shee teares, her head
>
> Was crownd with thornes, with dust besprinkeled;

Her loynes with sacke-cloth girt, her feete vncouered

[leaf 81, back] Repentance described by her closet.

By her actions.

By her attire.

141. (II. 34)

Angells stood round about her, as her gard,   1159

(Though to ye outwarde eye, they were not seene)

And what on earth was sayd, in heaun was hard,

And all her teares were kept in bottels cleane;

(Teares, though a signe, yet ease of sorrowes keene:)

> Her head was stayd by ye Angelique crewe,
>
> Who all besprinkled her with holy dewe,

That shee might neuer faint, but aye her plaints re-

newe.   1166

By her attendants.

142. (II. 35)

A Crystall¹ riuer swifte before her fled,   1167
(Noe other lookinge-glasse shee had, poore soule,)
Instead of waues, the teares lift vp y^r head,
And to ye muddy shore of sin they rowle,
Beatinge against ye rocke of scandalls fowle :   1171
   The water of it was exceedinge tarte,
   Sore to ye eyes, but saluinge to ye heart :
Thees streames, abundant teares to all sicke soules
   imparte.   1174

143. (II. 36)

Teares, ye Soules bath, ye weepinge oliue tree ;   1175
Teares, cause of comforte, though effect of greefe ;
Teares, heauens showers, ye dewe of Iris bee,
Teares, amonge Paradises riuers cheefe,
Teares, Pœnitences badge, and hearts releife ;   1179
   Teares bee ye sinner's solitary sporte ;
   Teares, hopefull sorrowe's longe-desired port ;
Teares, handmaides to Repentance in Astrœas courte.

144. (II. 37)

Repentance is ye way to life by death ;   1183
Repentance, health giu'n in a bitter pill ;
Repentance, hearbe of grace, diuiner breath ;
Repentance, rectifier of the will ;
Repentance, loue of good, and hate of ill ;   1187
   Repentance, mirth at last, though first annoy ;
   Repentance, Ibis, y^t doth snakes destroye ;
Repentance, earth's debate, heau'ns darlinge Angels
   ioye.   1190

145. (II. 38)

Teares quench ye thunder-bolts of zeale diuine,   1191
Repentance makes ye cruellst foe repent :
Teares keepe from putrefaction with y^r brine,
Repentance sharpe, but sweetend by content :

Teares earthly, yet vnto ye heauen[1] sent;   1195 and lead to
heaven.
 Repentance euer doth ye worke begin :   [1 MS. first
'heauns']
 Teares follow her, and cleanse ye sinke of sin :
Come, come, ye Saints, a pace! and with Repentance
 inne.   1198

146. (II. 39)

Desire's ye cause of Sin ; Sin, cause of greefe ;   1199 [leaf 82, back]
Greife bids repent, Repentance bringes forth teares ;   The cause of
Marie Magda-
lenes repent-
ance.
Teares, pitie mooue, and pitty graunts releife,
That comforte, comforte hope, which nothinge feares ;
Hope leades to faith, faith to ye Sauiour reares :   1203
 Iesus, to blisse, his militants doth raize ;
 Blisse causes glory, glory ends in prayse ;
Prayse ends in him, y^t no begininge knew, nor end of
 dayes.   1206

147. (II. 40)

This made ye Damsell in distressed state,   1207
Hopinge in teares to drench her misery,
Stand waitinge still at Pœnitence's gate :
Where, when shee knockt, Repentance by and by
Demaunded, whoe was there ; shee made replie : 1211
 A sinfull soule.—(*Rep.*) Then must you not come The true repent-
ance is a turninge
from sin.
  heere.
 (*Magdal.*) Oh, let me in (sweet Grace!) you need not
  feare.
(*Rep.*) Thou wilt defile my bridall chamber.—(*Mag.*)
 I am cleare.   1214

148. (II. 41)

(*Rep.*) Cleare? Whoe hath cleard thee, or with gracious
 light   1215
Illumined thy minde?—(*Magd.*) The holy one.
(*Rep.*) Where bee ye Spirits of Infernall night,
That whilome thee possest?—(*Mag.*) Oh; they are
 gone.

(*Repent.*) Where bee thy louers?—(*Mag.*) I am heere
alone.   1219

(*Rep.*) If I admit thee, wilt thou not repent?

Mary promises
to be firm in her
repentance.
(*Magd.*) Repent I neuer will.—(*Rep.*) To what intent
Should I then let thee in, if thou wilt n'er repent?

149. (II. 42)

[leaf 83]
(*Magd.*) Oh yes, I will repent me of my sin ;   1223
But of Repentance I will n'er repent.
(*Rep.*) What wilt thou doe, if y^t I let thee in?
(*Mag.*) With sorrowes due, I'll paye thee yearly rent.
(*Rep.*) What diœt wilt thou haue?—(*Mag.*) Sighes to
relent.   1227
(*Rep.*) They 're too stronge-breath'd.—(*Ma.*) Fitter
for my weake plaint.—
(*Rep.*) What more?—(*M.*) Fewe teares.   (*Rep.*) y^r
heat will make thee faint.
(*M.*) I freeze. (*Rep.*) They coulder are. (*M.*) I burne.
(*Rep.*) Come in, poore Saint !   1230

150. (II. 43)

Mary Magda-
lene repent-
ance.
Soe in shee came, directed by her guide,   1231
And dipt her finger in ye brinish[1] well,
[1 MS. brimish]
And with her eyes ye sharpnesse of it try'd,
In teares.
From whence ye teares, as thicke as showers, fell,
And raisd ye bubles of ye watry cell,   1235
As when a doubtfull cloud dissolus his raine,
Into ye ample bosome of ye maine :
His showers, her teares, y^t fell, seeme all to fall in
vaine.   1238

151. (II. 44)

In gesture.
Her head hunge downe, (heauy it was with greefe,)
Nor durst shee euer looke vp to ye skie :   1240
Of sinners shee esteem'd herselfe ye cheefe,
And knewe ye wrath of heauens maiesty.

Fast on y⁰ moystened floore, shee cast her eye,   1243
    And eu'ry where shee findes some cause to plaine,
    But still Syneide comforts her againe,   Conscience com-
And tells her, y^t y⁰ lambe, for sinners must bee slaine.   forts Mary.

152. (II. 45)

At length a rufull voice her silence brake,   1247   [leaf 83, back]
Like swellinge waters, troubled with y⁰ winde,
And thus with greefe of heart y⁰ Damsell spake,   In sorrowefull
"Ah, foolish woman, to thy selfe vnkinde!   eiaculations.
When others see, howe longe hast thou been blinde? 1251
    Witnesse y⁰ flash of pleasure for a while,
    That, with y⁰ falshehood of a guilded smile,
Did thee, poore wretch, allure; alluringe, did beguile.

153. (II. 46)

"Vaine pleasure, cause of endlesse paine, adieu! 1255   Conscience shows
Sweete is thy baite, but deadly is thy baine,   Mary the vanity
When for an howres delight, an age wee rue,   of Pleasure.
An ounce of mirth procures a world of paine,
And pleasure in his infancy is slaine: 1259
    The swellinge bubble, sweet flower, springinge grasse,
    Falls, fadeth, is not, what but now it was:
But shorter pleasure, all in shortnesse doth surpasse."

154. (II. 47)

Thus shee laments, and while shee casts her eyes 1263
Vpon y⁰ water, y^t was vnder placd,
Her gentle shadowe, mourninge shee espies,   In occasioninge
And all y⁰ beauty of her face defacd: 1266   of lamentation.
"Oh, hadst thou euer, (sayes shee) thus been grac'd,
    Beauty, thou rocke of Soules, faire Sirens smile,
    Nights glitteringe glowe-worme, wepinge Crocodile.
Beauty more lou'd then purest gould, then drosse more
        vile.   1270
        1268. Rawl. reads "Hellen's."

155. (II. 48)

[leaf 84]
" And yet ye pourtract of this outward frame,   1271
The rarest gifte, y^t euer from aboue
Heau'n did on earth bestowe, had not y^t shame
Of wretched man with-drawne his makers loue :
For, saue his soule infused by ye Doue,   1275
   What else in man worth note ?—vnhappy fall.
   Since when (but whoe can date expir'd recall ?)
That which is best in vs, wee make it worst of all. 1278

156. (II. 49)

In acknowledg-
inge her former
misdemeanor.
" Thees haires, y^t modestly should haue beene ty'd 1279
(For modesty 's a maydes best ornament)
Layd out in tresses, haue declar'd my pride :
Thees eyes were made to viewe ye firmament,
And giue Him glory, y^t such glory lent.   1283

Mary's eyes have
been wanton.
But (woe is mee !) they haue ye glasses beene,
   Where folly lookd, and wantonnesse was scene,
Soe ioyfull to attend vpon ye Cyprian Queene.   1286

157. (II. 50)

"Thees checkes should blush at sin with crimson die,
But they to lewdnesse cheefely doe inuite,

Her smiles have
tempted the
onlooker.
With smiles deceiuinge ye behoulders eye :
Thees lippes were made to prayse, and pray arright,
Not to delude ye soone-deluded sight :   1291
   This tongue should singe out Hallcluiahs,
   Not accent vaine lasciuious essayes :
Hands, feet, heart, all were made, to speake y^r makers
   prayse.   1294

158. (II. 51)

" But I (poore wretch ! such wretches, sinners bee), 1295
Led captiue by ye powers of Hell beneath,
Each member haue defild, noe parcell free,
And liuinge, entred in ye snares of death,

Vnworthy then to drawe this vitall breath.   1299

Oh that I might those yeares againe recall,

That made me free to Sin in Pleasures thrall."

Yet better late repente, then not repent at all :   1302

She wishes she could recall her ill-spent days.

159. (II. 52)

No siluer haires her goulden twist had chang'd,   1303

No pallid hue assaild her rosy-red,

No wrinkles had her browe from loue estraung'd,

No rottenesse her Iu'ry teeth be-spread :

Youth in his freshest colours flourished.   1307

And yet shee thought, in humblenesse of minde,

The dayes to longe, yᵗ had her thus confin'd,

Repentance, with yᵉ least offence, some falt can finde.

[leaf 84, back]

In humblenesse.

160. (II. 53)

Thus in her selfe, her selfe shee wellnigh lost,   1311

And on her selfe her sighes and sorrowes spent ;

Till yᵉ next roome her cogitations crost,

With pearly teares and Crystall[1] due besprent,

And gaue her store of matter to lament :   1315

Then shee begins a-fresh, (for to her thought

Thees spectacles yᵉ courts of Pleasure brought,

Where ill was counted good, and good was counted naught.)   1318

Mary weeps, and shows her repentance.

[1 MS. first 'Christall']

161. (II. 54)

" Faire courtes without, but foulest sinkes within, 1319

Vnder your roofes, would I had neuer beene !

Sweet sportes, but leauend with a lumpe of Sin !

Would God, I neuer had your madnesse seene !

And thou, vaine Pleasure, youths adored queene,   1323

Oh, maist thou euer bound in hell remaine,

And suffer torments of œternall paine !

For thou hast ship-wrackt all, and many a Soule hast slaine.   1326

In detesting of her sinfull life.

162. (II. 55)

"Better it is with-in this narrowe roome   1327
To spend our flittinge dayes, and closely keepe,
Then, while wee liue, soe fairely to intombe
Our soules in Marble pleasures, y* will weepe
Dayes without end, when wee haue tooke our sleepe.
    Better, this well of teares, then clearest founts,
    For sad Repentance, in true ioye surmounts
Vaine Pleasures shady bowers, sweet gardens, rich
        accounts.   1334

163. (II. 56)

"Better thy thorne-bush then a crowne of Myrtle, 1335
Thy ashes, better then y* bread of strife ;
Better thy sacke-cloth, then a silken kirtle ;
Thy bitter, better then y* sweetest life ;
Better thy selfe, then is y* rarest wife :   1339

    Repentance, hearts content, y* sinners stay,
    The salt of all our actions, y* key
That opens heau'n, and leads into y* courts of day. 1342

164. (II. 57)

"The hate of sinfull life, and sorrowes deepe,   1343
Surpasse y* loue of life, and life of loue :
For what is y* which wantons 'loue' yclepe,
But hot desires y* doe each passion mooue,
And through y* veines with lust-full poyson roaue ;
    A foolish fancy and a pleasinge paine,
    That dimmes y* eyes, and dulls y* purest braine. 1349
But loue, from heauen came, and thither goes againe."

165. (II. 58)

So nowe, me thinkes, her waylinge should be done, 1351
The closets shutt, y* liquid fountaine drie ;
Herselfe, loue, pleasure, shee hath ouer-run,
Yet downe her cheekes y* Isicles doe hie,

Though sad laments and waylinge accents die :   1355
  Sighes serue for voice, teares for a tongue, to showe
  The meaninge of her minde, and inward woe :   *and goes out with Repentance.*
And when all 's done, abroad shee and Repentance goe.

166. (II. 59)

And as they walke abroad in open aire,   1359
Each thinge shee spies, is matter of her teares :
The creatures with her-selfe shee doth compare ;   *In contempla-tion.*
And when yᵉ Sun in bright array appeares,
He blushes at her shame ; and when shee heares   1363
  The chirpinge birds, she thinkes they doe reioyce
  To see her weepe, and heare her broken voice ;
And vpon her alone, yᵉ beasts to gaze make choyse.

167. (II. 60)

As by she passes, each tree shakes his head,   1367   *All Nature seems to reproach Mary.*
Notinge her shame, and infamy of life :
The flowers turne, and seeme refuse her tread ;
The buzzinge flies about are very rife ;
The winde, against her, blowes with mickle strife :
  But to herselfe most sharpe, she rents her haire,
  Showringe forth teares, with sighes and humble   *Ioyn'd with sighes and prayer.*
    prayer,
So to content yᵉ earth with teares, with sighes yᵉ aire.

168. (II. 61)

Then a newe contemplation shee invents,   1375   *[leaf 86]*
(But all her contemplations holy were,)
And thus with piteous mone shee sore laments,
Holdinge her hands vp to yᵉ spangled sphære :
"Oh thou yᵗ guidst thy burninge horses there,   1379
  Thy state I envie, sith thy race is run
  From East to West, and mine scarse yet begun ;
My darknesse, others blindes ; to others, shines yᵉ
    Sun.

169. (II. 62)

She contrasts its
sweet scents

" Sweete is ye smell, y^t fragrant flowers bringe,   1383
Wouinge ye winde to kisse them once againe;
Sweet are ye notes, y^t birds sit carolinge
To him y^t made them; but ye filthy staine

with her foul sin.

Of sin hath mee disodour'd, and my straine   1387
Tunes nought but vanity and fond delight:
The grasse with freshest colours is bedight;
The trees bringe fruit: but fruitlesse I, as darke as
   night.   1390

170. (II. 63)

"The fire hath heat, but I was dead in sin: 1391
The aire is moist, my vertue withered:
Solid ye earth: but I haue euer been
Vnstable: water coole; I, tortured

[leaf 86, back]

With burninge lust: All haue perseuered   1395

Nature has
obeyed God.
Mary has wrought
only ill.

   In true obedience, performinge still,
   What was inioyn'd them first by heauens will,
While I, vnhappy soule, haue wrought no worke but [ill.]

171. (II. 64)

"Oh that mine eyes a fountaine weare of teares,   1399

In her wishes.

That I might cleanse my sin-polluted soule,
Or y^t my dayes were like ye Eagles yeares,
That with my age I might renewe my smarte,
So should Repentance neuer from mee parte!"   1403
   But oh, enough (faire Damsell), though ye skies
   Nor ye vast sea with water can suffice
To purge our sin, yet faith from heauen biddes thee rise."

172. (II. 65)

Mary hears that
Jesus is at the
Pharisee's house.

So shee arrose, and by ye way heard tell,   1407
That Iesus with ye Pharise nowe sate:
Thrice happy messenger, y^t came so well,
Such vnexpected tidinges to relate,

And helpe a sinner in distress'd estate !　　　1411
　　Yet shee was daunted at yᵉ Pharise,
　　(For Pharises and sinners n'er agree,
Though Pharises themselues, of s[i]nners cheefest bee).

173. (II. 66)

A while shee pauzinge stood, and 'gan to doubt,　1415　[leaf 87]
Whither shee to yᵉ Pharises should goe,　　　　　She doubts whe-
　　　　　　　　　　　　　　　　　　　　　　　ther she should
Or rather for her Sauiour staye without;　　　　go there.
(Such men bee of austere regarde, wee knowe,
And to yᵉ vulgar make a goodly showe.)　　　　1419
　　But other thoughts, to quell this care begin,
　　"The Pharise's a man, and men haue sin ;
Then, bee hee n'er so good, a better is within.　　1422

174. (II. 67)

" A better is within, and hee so good,　　　　　1423
That howe maye I, polluted soule, come neare ?
Women defiled with a fluxe of blood,
Maye not amonge yᵉ hallowed appeare :
I am vnclean, and leprous eu'ry where,　　　　1427　She is unclean.
　　How shall I then approach before his eye,
　　More bright then is [yᵉ] Eagle's, yᵗ doth prie
Into yᵉ cabinets of deepest secrecy ?—　　　　　1430

175. (II. 68)

"But yet in mercy is his cheefe delight :　　　　1431　[leaf 87, back]
Hee came to heale yᵉ sicke, to saue yᵉ lost ;　　Mary recounts
　　　　　　　　　　　　　　　　　　　　　　the good deeds of
Hee cur'd 10 Lepres, gaue yᵉ blinde yʳ sight,　　Jesus.
Feet to yᵉ lame, life to yᵉ nummed ghost,
Speech to yᵉ dumbe, and comforte to yᵉ moste :　1435
　　And, which with prayse must euer bee confest,
　　(Blest be yᵉ time ! his name for euer blest !)
Seu'n sprights, with thunder hee ycharm'd from out my
　　　　brest.　　　　　　　　　　　　　　　　1438

176. (II. 69)

"Certes his loue will couer all my shame,   1439
And with his robe my errours I may hide:
For I am sicke, lost, leprous, blinde, and lame,
Dumbe, comforteles, and dead: nor is it pride,
To seeke for helpe: then, what so'er betide,   1443
   Thither I'l goe! if Christ once bidde me stay,
   The Pharise can neuer say mee nay:
Oh, happy place, where heau'n hath placd another day!"

She resolves to go to Him at the Pharisee's.

177. (II. 70)

A boxe of costely odours shee præpar'd,   1447
Odours t' anoynt[1] th' anoynted from aboue,
And with it streight to Simons house shee far'd,
With true repentance to declare her loue:
Shee brake it, and y̑ roome could soone approoue 1451
   The fragrant smell: such is a contrite heart,
   That to y̑ heau'n sweet sauours doth impart,
The oyntment of good workes, and pænitence, ne'r parte.

[leaf 88]
[1 H. anotnt]
In her charity.

178. (II. 71)

Præpared thus, behinde his feet shee stood,   1455
Dissolu'd in teares of sweet (though bitter) brine,
And with y̑ torrent of a Chrystall[1] flood,
Shee wash'd his feet, his iu'ry feet diuine,
And then shee wip'd them with y̑ goulden twine 1459
   Of her dissheuel'd haires: full many a kisse
   Shee gaue, and tooke; and, conscious of y̑ʳ blisse,
Her lippes waxt pale, for feare they had done ought
   amisse.   1462

Luk: 7: 38:
In her behauiour.
[1 MS. first 'Christall']
Mary washes Christ's feet: wipes them with her hair, and kisses them.

179. (II. 72)

That falt, y̑ willinge maide will soon amend,   1463
For lauishely shee powres her oyntment sweet,
(Though lauishely enough shee n'er could spend
That which shee spent vpon his heau'nly feet:)

[leaf 88, back]
Then she anoints them.

So did her misery his mercy greet: 1467
   Sweet was thy vnction (Mary), sweet thy kisse,
   But sweetest of all sweetes, thy teares (I-wis):
The onely waye to heauen, by salt water is.   1470

180. (II. 73)

Happy wert thou to touch ye tressells bare   1471   Happy she to
Of thy beloued, heau'nly paramour,   touch and kiss
                                         her Saviour's
With eye, with hand, with temples, lippe and haire: body so!
Yet thrice more happy, sith thy Sauiour,
With eye, heart, hand of faith thou didst adore: 1475
   So doth a loue-sicke soule of best desarte,
   Desire to touch her louer in each part,
And closely steale his body, y^t hath stole her heart.

181. (II. 74)

Oyntement shee mingles aye with bitter teares;   1479   [leaf 89]
Teares with sweet oyntement aye shee doth confound: She sheds bitter
No better balme in Gilead appeares,   teares.
No sweeter smell in Lebanous rich ground:
This saints ye sinner, makes ye sickest sound: 1483
   Oyntement and teares (if true) to get her inne,
   First ope ye sluce, and shed teares for thy sin,
Then to anoynt Christe's feet, with Magdalen begin. 1486

182. (II. 75)

Humility, lowe at his feet biddes stand;   1487   Reflections on
Behinde him, rosy-blushinge Modesty: Mary's acts.
Teares for his feet, Repentance doth commaund;
And Selfe-Hate, with her haire biddes make them drie:
Loue biddes her kisse, and Liberality   1491
   Wills her to breake ye boxe, and oyntement powre.
   Hardenes of heart, pride, shamelesnesse before,
Lust, luxury, selfe-loue, possess'd her thoughts of yore.

183. (II. 76)

Mee thinkes, I see yᵉ Damsell at her worke,   1495
While shee embalmes his feet with odours rare ;
With modest blush, howe shee hath learnt to lurke,
And kisse his feet, his marble feet, so faire,
And then to wipe them with her carelesse haire : 1499
Often her hands, often her lippes, came near[e] ;
Oft wipes shee of yᵉ oyntment, yᵗ I feare,
The oyntement wanted sweet, his feet perfumed weare.

184. (II. 77)

Yet sweet yᵉ oyntement was, though sweeter farre 1503
The Nectar of his feet, with dewe besprent :
So weake perfumes (though sweet) soone drowned are,
If they bee mingled with a deper sent :
Simons good cheare giues no such good content : 1507
His ghuests are frolicke with yʳ dainty meat ;
But shee delights yᵉ brinish teares to eat,
And ioyeth more in hers, then they in highest seat. 1510

185. (II. 78)

Some at feast haue crau'd thy company ;   1511
But fewe or none, sweet oyntment for thee kept ;
Some haue anoynted, but fewe wip'd the[e] drie :
Some wip'd thee drie ; but wipinge, fewe haue wept ;
Beyond them all, kinde Magdalene hath stept : 1515
Some on thy head bestow'd yʳ charity,
(Such was yᵉ vse in auncient times,) but shee,
Oyntinge thy feet, from toppe to toe anoynted thee. 1518

186. (II. 79

O, that I might, with waueringe Thomas, dippe 1519
The finger of mý faith within his side,
Or heere with Magdalene obtaine a sippe,
(Farre from my humble thought bee greater pride !)

From out his feet, with pleasures beautified ;   1523
  What would hee giue for weepinge Maries place,   Lips: in theatr:
  Whose hermitinge humility could grace   honor: Iesuit:
The Linnen cloutes, y^t did our Sauiours wound embrace.

187. (II. 80)

Faine would I leaue of Maries loue to writ[e],   1527   I must write still
                                                                              of Mary's love.
But still her loue y^t will not let me leaue :
In loue shee liu'd, and now with loues delight,
Her former loue, y^t did her eyes decciue,
In-stead of loue, of life shee doth bereaue :   1531
  Faire mayde, redeemed from ye iawes of Hell,
  Howe hardly can I bidde thy loue fare-well !
That which thou lou'st to doe, so doe I loue to tell. 1534

188. (II. 81)

The Pharisæ y^t thought hee sawe, was blinde ;   1535   [leaf 90, back]
The abiect sinner had the clearer eye ;
For thus hee reasoned within his minde ;
' Were this a Prophet, hee would soone descrie   Simon doubts
                                                                               Jesus being a
The wickednesse of her y^t standes so nighe : '   1539   Prophet.
  Thus hee coniectur'd, yet hee vtter'd nought :
  But his hypocrisie to light was brought ;
For well hee knewe her former life, y^t knewe his
      thought.   1542

189. (II. 82)

Then hee begins her action to commend   1543
To Simon in a parable of debt,
And sayes vnto him : " Seest thou her, my freind ?   Jesus shows
                                                                               Simon how Mary's
Great is her loue, because her Sin is great :   love exceeds his.
To washe my feet, no water hast thou set ;   1547
  But shee with teares hath washt them : on my head
  Thou hast not powred oyle : but shee, in-stead,
With costly oyntement hath my feet be-sprinkeled. 1550
MARY MAGDALENE.
                                                                      F

190. (II. 83)

"No kisse thou gau'st mee for a kinde salute ;   1551
But shee vnto my feet doth kisses giue :
So her affection with her smiles doe sute :

Jesus pardons and blesses Mary. Thy sinns (sayth hee) are cleansd, and thou shalt liue :
Goe hence in peace, sweete mayde ! for euer thriue !"
    Wonder it is, y^t hee, whose sacred might   1556
    May call all prayse and glory, his by right,
Should giue such heaunly prayse vnto a mortall wight.

191. (II. 84)

[leaf 91] Away shee went, aggladded at the heart,   1559
(Packe hence all sorrowe, let ye Damsell cheare !)
. Yet so, y^t neuer from him shee would parte :
And nowe her browe and cheekes began to cleare,
And ioye displayd his banners eu'ry where ;   1563
    Now with a shole of Maries so deuout,

In her religious duties.   Shee ministers, and deales her goods about,
And followes her Leige-Lorde ye villages throughout.

192. (II. 85)

Nowe on his rarest miracles shee gazeth,   1567
And with attention shee likes to heare,
While hee ye lustre of his light eblazeth,

Mary listens to all Christ says. And charmes with sacred cloquence each eare.
So shee awaited still, both farre and neare,   1571
    Till death approach'd, and hee inuaded Hell :
    But of his death, what should I further tell ?
Better maye hee that sauge his birth, ringe out his knell.

193. (II. 86)

Many a teare in Golgotha shee spent,   1575
To waile his torment and her owne distresse ;

Mary anoints Christ's corpse. And after, hied her to his monument,
With odours sweet his wounded corps to dresse :

        1566. *throughout :* Rawl. about.

In life shee lou'd him, and in death no lesse.   1579
   The earth was clad with sable weeds of night
   When Magdalene, so full of rufull plight,
Prœuents y⁰ daye, and in y⁰ darke seekes for her light.   Joh: 20: 1:

194. (II. 87)

O blessed woman, without Paragon,   1583   [leaf 91, back]
That couldst outrun (such is y⁰ force of loue)
The faithefull Peter and beloued Iohn,
And bee y⁰ first y¹ sawe y⁰ stones remoue !
This boone was graunted thee from heau'n aboue : 1587   Her loue to
   But when shee could not finde his body there,   Christe, and
   Shee runs to them, and cries with piteous feare,   sorrowe for his
      death.
" Aye mee ! my lord is gon ! and layd, wee knowe not
     where."   1590

195. (II. 88)

Iohn faster ran, but Peter farther went :   1591
Hee came vnto y⁰ sepulchre, and stayd ;
The other entred in y⁰ monument ;
But both out-stripped by y⁰ weepinge mayde :
They sawe y⁰ linnen clothes and kercheife layd   1595
   A-part : but shee, y⁰ Angells first did viewe,   Mary sees the
   As downe shee bow'd, in weeds of whitest hue.   Angels first.
Poore Mary knewe not them, although they   Mary
   knewe.   1598

196. (II. 89)

Shee drownes her-selfe in teares of saltest brine ; 1599
They aske her, why shee weepes, and makes such mone :
Shee sayes, " my Lorde is taken from this shrine ; "
And hauing sayd, shee spies her Lord alone ;
And yet to her, though seen, hee is not knowne : 1603
   " Woman ! (sayes hee) why makst thou such laments ? "
   Shee aunswerd, " Sir ! if thou hast borne him hence,   Mary asks Christ
      where her Lord is
Tell mee but where hee lies, and I will fetch him thence."   laid.

1580. H. and R. read "might," which I suppose is a mistake of the copyist.

197. (II. 90)

Shee thought her Lorde, ye gardiner had been :   1607
And keeper of a garden, sure, was hee :
Yet no such garden, where dead sculls are seen,
But Paradise, where pleasures euer bee,
And blisse deriu'd from lifes aye-liuinge tree :   1611
   Thither ye theife and he together went,
   And thither Mary must at length bee sent ;
But first ye dimme light of her life must needs bee spent.

198. (II. 91)

Shee, to anoynt his breathlesse body came ;   1615
With oyle of gladnesse hee, to oynt her head :
To keepe him from corruption, was her ayme ;
His purpose was to raise her from ye dead.

Christ calls her
by her name.

By name hee call'd her (happily shee sped !)   1619
   To bee the messenger of heau'[n]ly newes,
   That gladdes the heart, and fadinge age renewes,
And to ye Saints, thinges longe time vnreueiled shewes.

199. (II. 92)

She tells the
Saints that He
has risen.

Awaye shee postes, all rauish'd with desire,   1623
And to ye Saints together met, shee hies :
Her tidings make ye trobled soules admire ;
And yet her solace, and sweet obloquies,
Make constant hope, and better thoughts arrise.   1627
   Their prayses loud vp to y^e heau'ns they send :

All rejoice.

   Ioye closes all, (such ioye no style hath penn'd)
So end I with y^r ioye ; ner may y^t ioye haue end !   1630

$$\Delta \acute{o} \xi a \; \tau \tilde{\omega} \; \vartheta \epsilon \tilde{\omega}.$$

DE CHRISTO CUM SIMONE PHARISÆO PRANDENTE, [leaf 93]
ET MARIAM MAGDALENAM COMITER EXCIPIENTE.

Quid petit angustas epulas Simonis Iesus,
 Qui sua Nectareis proluit ora cadis?
Non opus est illi mortalibus: ille tuetur,
 Quicquid habet tellus, æquora quicquid habent:
Forsitan haud cupiit ditis conviuia mensæ,
 Sed cupiit lacrymas præscius (alma) tuas:
Credo, insulsa forent tua nam conuiuia Simon,
 Magdala in tepidum funderet vsque salem.

FLET: RIDET.

AD MARIAM MAGDALENAM.

Cum video risum porrecta fronte serenum,
 Cum video lacrymas (alma puella) tuas,
Sic reputo: certè omen habet, seu riserit amens
 Magdala, sine etiam Magdala fleuit amans:
Sunt avi violenta breuis: nam gaudia luctum
 Tanta ferunt, tántus gaudia luctus habet:
Vt fleat alternum, mihi sic risisse videtur,
 Sic. flere, vt tandem rideat illa magis.

AD EANDEM.

Magdala, quid miserè lacrymarum flumina fundis? [leaf 95, back]
 Perfundis liquido quid tibi rore genas?
Abluis anne pedes Domini? sed sorde carebant;
 Abluis au culpam (non caret illâ) tuam?
An sic Angelicos vtres implere requiris?
 An sic cœlestes pura videbis aquas?
O sale macte tuo: tibi Spiritus, aura fecunda est,
 Anchora, spes audax, carbasa, laeta fides.
T. R.

Laus Deo.

NOTES.

40. *Persius*, Flaccus Aulus, a Latin poet of Volaterræ, was of an
equestrian family, and made himself known by his intimacy with the
most illustrious Romans of the age. He distinguished himself by
satirical humour, and made the faults of the orators and poets of his
time the subject of his poems. He died A.D. 62.

52. *Harrington*, James, an eminent political writer, was born in
1611, being the eldest son of Sir Lapcote Harrington. When he made
progress in classical learning, he was admitted, in 1629, a gentleman-
commoner of Trinity College, Oxford, etc. He made some attempts in
the poetical way. In 1658 he published an English translation of two
eclogues of Virgil, and two books of the *Æneis*, and in 1659 was printed
his translation of the four following books of the *Æneis*; but his poetry
gained him no reputation as his political writings did. See *Biographica
Britannica; Athen. Oxon.* vol. ii., and Chalmers's *Biograph. Dictionary.*

64. *Aratus*, a Greek poet of Cilicia; about 277 B.C. He was greatly
esteemed by Antigonus Gonatus, king of Macedonia, at whose court he
passed much of his time, and at whose request he wrote a poem on
astronomy, comprehended in 1154 verses, in which he gives an account
of the situations, rising, setting, number, and motion of the stars.
Cicero represents him as unacquainted with astrology, yet capable of
writing upon it in elegant and highly-finished verses, which, however,
from the subject, admit of little variety. Aratus wrote also hymns and
epigrams, etc.

St. Paul, when addressing the philosophers of Athens in the Areo-
pagus, quotes the exordium of Aratus's *Phenomena* (Acts xvii. 28. For
in him we live, and move, and have our being: as certain also of *your
own poets have said,* For we are also his offspring). "Although the
sacred historian only gives four words as a reference to the passage, it
is likely that St. Paul quoted some more, to prove to his learned audience
that the doctrine of the eternity, unity, and omnipotence of the Godhead
was no new invention, or confined to the Jewish nation, but the creed
of the wisest of their own philosophers and poets."

English translations of his works are: a. Jabez Hughes, Translations
from Aratus in his *Miscellanies in Prose and Verse.* Lond. 1737. β *The
Phenomena and Diosemeia*, translated into English verse, with notes, by
J. Lamb. Lond. 1848. γ. *The Skies and Weather Forecasts of Aratus*,
translated, with notes, by E. Poste. Lond. 1880.

66. *Lucan*, Roman poet of the Augustan age, died A.D. 65.

88. *Chrysostom[e]*, a bishop of Constantinople, who died A.D. 407, in his 53rd year. He was a great disciplinarian, and by severely lashing the vices of his age, he procured himself many enemies. He was banished for opposing the raising a statue to the Empress Eudoxia, the wife of Arcadius, after having displayed his abilities as an elegant preacher, a sound theologian, and a faithful interpreter of Scripture. His works appeared in 1718 in 13 vols. fol., Paris, ed. Benedict. Mountfaucon.

89. *Prudentius*, Aurelius Clemens, a Latin poet, who flourished A.D. 392, and was successively a soldier, an advocate, and a judge. His poems are numerous, and all theological, devoid of the elegance and purity of the Augustan age, and yet greatly valued for the zeal which he manifests in the cause of Christianity, and for the learning and good sense which he everywhere displays. He lived a great age, and his piety was rewarded by the highest offices in the Church. His works appeared at Paris, 1687, ed. The Delphin.

β. NOTES TO "THE LIFE AND DEATH OF MARY MAGDALENE."

4. *debellish* = embellish (Fletcher).

7. *spiny* = thorny.

12. *needs* is here the old adverb *necessarily*

41. *greeces*: obs. term for steps.

54. *Alcides*: a name of Heracles, either from his strength (ἀλκή) or from his grandfather *Alcœus*.

64. *in lue of*, in lewe of = au lieu de.

69. *Falern*: on the south-west coast of Italy, famous for its wine.

70. *Thyme of Hybla*: Hybla (major) near the south of Ætna, on a hill of the same name as the city; near it ran the Limœthus; famous for honey and bees.

Libyan flowers. Libya is the name given by the Greek and Roman poets to what is otherwise called Africa; in a more restricted sense applied to the two countries of Cyrenica and Marmarica.

71. *Tagus*: Tajo river in Portugal.

83. *streight* or strait = narrowly. *amaine* = violently.

175. *Lapithœ*: Lapithus, son of Apollo by Stilbe, brother of Centaurus.

178. *iarre* = eare, heare. *Stratmann Dict.*, p. 334.

203. Rhodope, a high mountain in Thrace.

251. Astrœa, a daughter of Astrœus, king of Arcadia, or according to others of Titan, Saturn's brother, by Aurora; some make her daughter of Jupiter and Themis. She was called Justice as a goddess of virtue, and lived on the earth during the golden age; the impiety of mankind drove her to heaven in the brazen and iron ages, and she was placed as Virgo among the constellations of the zodiac.

304. Atlas, a Titan, son of Japetus and Clymene, one of the Oceanides, brother of Promethcus.

305. *Heloriz:* Helorus (Abiso), a river of Sicily near the southern extremity of the island; mentioned by several ancient poets for the remarkably fertile country through which it flows. Virgil, *Æneid*, iii. 659; Ovid, *Fast.*, iv. 487.

306. Alcinous, a son of Nausithous, king of Phæacia, praised for his love of agriculture; he is the same that entertained Ulysses. Homer beautifully describes his gardens on the island of Sheria (Corfu or Corcyra).

351. *pillastrells*, from the Ital. *pillastrello.*

364. *ramillets*, from the Spanish *ramillete*, means: 1. A bunch of divers flowers and herbs tied together. 2. A collection of exquisite and useful thoughts on any subject.

Posy. 1. Motto inscribed on a ring. (Addison.) 2. A bunch of flowers. (Spenser.)

427. Lynceus, a son of Alpharcus, among the hunters of the Caledonian boar, one of the Argonauts. He was so sharp-sighted, that it is reported he could see through the earth and distinguish objects at nine miles. Palaeph., 57; Pliny, ii. xvii.

451. *Gnossian Crowne:* Gnossis, Gnossia, an epithet given to Ariadne, because she lived or was born at Gnossus; the crown which she received from Bacchus, and which was made a constellation: Gnossia stella. Virgil, G. i. 222.

459—461. Hieronymus Zanchius: De operibus Dei intra spatium sex diorum creatis; Hanoviæ 1597, lib. 2, cap. 6. Thesis: Nemo Angelorum creatus fuit a Deo malus, sed omnes ex æquo boni; verum, sicut omnes intellectu ad cognoscendum prœditi, sic etiam omnes voluntate ad eligendum, vel repudiandum liberi. Quare quod quidam illorum mali sint, hoc a se ipsis, non autem ex Deo habere.

582. *to cark* = to care in v. Esmay. Cf. Collier's *Old Ballads*, p. 38. F. carko = *je chagrine.* Palsgrave.

620. Phyllis, a daughter of Sitho, or according to others of Lycurgus, king of Thrace, hospitably received Demophro, son of Theseus, who at his return from the Trojan war had stopped on her coasts; became enamoured of him, and he was not insensible of her passion. After some months of mutual tenderness and affection, Demophro set sail for Athens, where his domestic affairs recalled him; promised faithfully to return as soon as a month was expired. His dislike for Phyllis, or the irreparable situation of his affairs, obliged him to violate his engagement, and Phyllis, desperate from his absence, hanged herself. Ovid, *Her.*, II. ii. 353; *Trist.*, ii. 437; Virgil, Eclogue III.

623. Pyramus, a youth of Babylon, became enamoured of Thisbe, a beautiful virgin who dwelt in the vicinity; the flame was mutual, and the two lovers, whom their parents forbade to marry, regularly received each other's addresses through the chink of a wall which separated their houses. After the most solemn vows of sincerity, they both agreed to

clude the vigilance of their friends, and meet one another on the tomb of Ninus, under a white mulberry-tree, without the walls of Babylon. Thisbe came first to the appointed place, but the sudden arrival of a lioness frightened her away; and as she fled into a neighbouring cave, dropped her veil, which the lioness found and besmeared with blood. Pyramus soon found Thisbe's veil all bloody, and concluding that she had been torn to pieces by the wild beasts of the place, stabbed himself with his sword. Thisbe, when her fears were vanished, returned from the cave, and at the sight of dying Pyramus, fell on the sword reeking with his blood. This happened under a mulberry-tree, which, as the poets mention, was stained with the blood of the lovers, and ever after bore fruit of the colour of blood. Ovid, *Met.*, iv. 55.

629. Empedocles, a philosopher, poet, and historian of Agrigentum, in Sicily, flourished in 444; he was the disciple of Telanges the Pythagorean, and warmly adopted the doctrine of transmigration. His curiosity to inspect the crater of Ætna proved fatal to him; some maintain that he wished to pass for a god, and, that his death might be unknown, threw himself into the crater; his expectations were frustrated, the volcano threw up one of his sandals, and discovered to the world that he perished by fire.

630. Stagirite, surname of Aristotle, from the city of Stagira in Macedonia, on the western shore of the Sinus Strymonicus (Gulf of Contessa), founded 665, and native place of Aristotle.

642. *sagge* = to hang down heavily (North). "Sir Rowland Russet-coat, goes sagging everie day in his round gascoynes of white cotton." —*Pierce Penilesse*, 1592.

698. *Cocyte* (Cocytus), a river of Epirus, blends its nauseous waters with those of the Achero; *Paus.*, I. 17. Its etymology, the unwhole-someness of its waters, and its vicinity to the Achero, have made the poets call it a river of hell; hence Cocytia virgo, applied to Alecto, one of the Furies. *Virg.*, G. III. 38; IV. 479. *Æneis*, VI. 297, 323; VII. 479.

700. *scritch* = to shriek (Devonshire).

711. Amphitrite, daughter of Oceanus and Thetis, married Neptune, though he had made a vow of perpetual celibacy; she had a statue at Corinth in the temple of Neptune, sometimes called Salaria, often taken for the sea itself. Ovid, *Met.*, i. 14.

720, 722. It looks, at first, as if these lines needed transposing; but the point is, that the folk in Hell suffer at the same moment both intense heat and intense cold, and yet neither of these affords any relief to its opposite.

759—66. H. Zanchius, De operibus, etc., lib. 4, cap. 19. Thesis: Dæmones sive præditi sint corporibus, sive non præditi: Tamen præter spiritualem montis et voluntatis multiplicem afflictionem, tor-mentum etiam ac dolorem, et nunc a multis rebus corporeis pati, idque mirabilibus modis possibile est atque probabile: Et postmodum a fine seculi usque in sempiternum passuros esse ab igne Gebennali necesse est.

767. Cimmerii, a people near the Palus Mæotis; invaded Asia

Minor, and seized on the kingdom of Cyaxares; masters of the country for 28 years; driven back by Algathes, king of Lydia (Herod., I. vi. 4). They seem to have been a northern nation driven from their abodes by the Scythians, and compelled to seek for new habitations; Posidonius makes them of Cimbric or German origin. Their first appellation is not known; that of Cimmerii they are said to have obtained after inhabiting the town of Cimmerium and its vicinity on the Cimmerian Bosporus. This seems improbable, as it is more natural to suppose that they gave name to the town and strait. The country bordering on the Palus Mæotis and Bosporus, inhabited by the Cimmerii, is represented by the ancients as inhospitable and black, covered with forests and fogs, impenetrable for the sun; hence, according to some, arose the expression Cimmerian darkness. Homer places his Cimmerium beyond the Oceanus, in a land of continual gloom, and immediately after them the empire of the shades.

773. *Leviathan* (Hebrew): water animal mentioned in the book of Job, by some imagined to be the crocodile, but in poetry generally taken for the whale. No known animal answers to it exactly. Shakspere mentions it in *Henry V.*, III. iii. Compare Job xii.

789. *fecche* = to fetch.

815. Cynthus (Monte Cintio), a mountain of Delos. Apollo was surnamed Cynthius; Diana, Cynthia; as born on the mountain sacred to them. Virgil, G. iii. 36 ; Ovid, *Met.*, vi. 304.

818. Cynosure (Cape Cavala), a promontory of Attica, formed by the range of Pentelicus.

820. Phlegetho, a river of hell whose waters were burning. Virgil, *Æneid*, vi. 550; Ovid, *Met.*, xv. 532.

829. Tityus, a giant, son of Terra, according to others of Jupiter by Elara, daughter of Orchomenos, was of such a prodigious size, that his mother died in travail after Jupiter had drawn her from the bowels of the earth, where she had been concealed during her pregnancy, to avoid the anger of Juno. Ovid, *Met.*, iv. 457.

834. Ixion, king of Thessaly, was tortured in hell by being tied to a wheel which was continually whirling round. Virgil, *Æneid*, vi. 601 ; Ovid, *Met.*, xii. 210, 338.

870. Vergellus, a small river near Cannæ, falling into the Aufidus, over which Hannibal (the Punicki) made a bridge with the slaughtered bodies of the Romans. Flor., ii. 6.

871. Perillus, an artist of Athens, made a brazen bull for Phalaris, tyrant of Agrigentum. This machine was fabricated to put criminals to death by burning them alive, and it was said that their cries were like the roaring of a bull. When Perillus gave it to Phalaris, the tyrant made the first experiment on him, and cruelly put him to death by lighting a slow fire under the belly of the bull. . Pliny, xxxiv. 8; Ovid, *A. A.*, i. 439, 653.

959—966. H. Zanchius, De operibus, etc., lib. 3, cap. 9. Thesis: Quæ in nobis sunt cogitationes, desideria et affectus, nisi per externa vel affecta, vel signa sese utcumque prodant, vel a Deo revelentur : cognosci ab Angelis minime possunt. lib. 4, cap. 9. (The manuscript gives wrongly lib. 9, for the book contains but five chapters.) Thesis : Dæmones nullas hominis cogitationes certo et per se cognoscere possunt ; sed multas per externa signa et probabiliter percipere valent.

1011. Panopœ, one of the Nereides, whom sailors generally invoked in storms. Virgil, *Æneid*, v. 825.

1124. Castalus fons in Syria, near Daphne ; the waters believed to give a knowledge of futurity to those who drank them. The oracle at the fountain promised Hadrian supreme power when he was yet in a private station ; he had the fountain shut up with stones when he ascended the throne.

1574. "*Better maye hee that sange his birth, ringe out his knell.*" The Singer of Christ's birth, referred to in this line, is doubtless Thomas Becon (or Beacon), born about 1512 in Norfolk or Suffolk, and died in 1567 or 1570. He is a contemporary of, and most likely a man well known to, Robinson. I have mentioned in the introduction that Robinson belonged to the divines who were ordered to assist Bishop Cranmer in the compilation of the Book of Common Prayer. Becon was Cranmer's chaplain, and Prebendary of Canterbury ; he was a learned divine, and published a great number of writings of a religious character, which appeared in three folio volumes in 1560—4. News about his life may be gained from—1. Lupton's *History of the Modern Protestant Divines.* Lond. 1637. 2. The Biographies prefixed to the late selections of his writings published by the Religious Tract Society (*British Reformers.* Lond. 1828—31), and by the Society for Promoting Christian Knowledge (*Selections from the Works of Thomas Becon.* Lond. 1839). 3. Several particulars may also be gleaned from *Fox* and *Strype.* A complete list of his numerous writings is to be found in Tanner's *Bibliotheca Britannica.* The Rev. John Ayre, M.A., republished most of Becon's works in 1844 (Cambridge) for the Parker Society, and prefixed to his edition the little that is known about Becon's life. The poem in question is entitled : "A newe Dialoge betwene thangel of god and the Shepherds of ye felde concerning the nativite & byrth of Iesus Christ our Lord and savior, no lesse Godly than swete and pleasante to reade, lately compyled by Thomas Becon." It is the only known poetical work of the author, and not yet republished ; it appears that it is very little known, and even Allibone does not mention it under Becon. The first stanza runs :

> A swete message
> To euery age
> From God so sage
> Is gyuen to me :
> Whiche to declare
> Both nere and fare
> To exclude care
> Glad wolde I be, etc.

INDEX OF NAMES, WORDS, AND SUBJECTS.

The numbers refer to the pages (and lines, when like 10/33) in the text.

Words marked by an asterisk (*) are to be found in the notes.

www.ingramcontent.com/pod-product-compliance
Lightning Source LLC
Chambersburg PA
CBHW022344020726
47500CB00004B/1271